THE SECRET OF THE RED TRUCK

The Secret of the Red Truck

Kyler James

REBEL SATORI PRESS
Bar Harbor • New Orleans

Published in the United States of America by
REBEL SATORI PRESS
P.O. Box 363
Hulls Cove, ME 04644
www.rebelsatori.com

This is a work of fiction. Names, characters, places, and incidents are the product of the author's imagination and are used fictitiously and any resemblance to actual persons, living or dead, business establishments, events, or locales is entirely coincidental. The publisher does not have any control over and does not assume any responsibility for author or third-party websites or their content.

Book design by Sven Davisson
Cover photograph by Mark Poprocki

Library of Congress Cataloging-in-Publication Data

James, Kyler, 1953-
  The secret of the red truck : a novel / Kyler James.
    page cm.
  ISBN 978-1-60864-105-5 (pbk. : alk. paper)
  1. Brothers and sisters--Fiction. 2. Truck drivers--Fiction. 3. Triangles (Interpersonal relations)--Fiction I. Title.
  PS3610.A4465S43 2014
  813'.6--dc23
                        2014016611

for my mother and my father

Why should one fear the voices of children?
It is for love they cry, my lord, more than for guidance.

— Gian Carlo Menotti
The Death of the Bishop of Brindisi

There is *only* a perspective seeing, *only* a perspective "knowing";
and the *more* affects we allow to speak about one thing, the *more* eyes,
different eyes, we can use to observe one thing, the more complete will
our "concept" of this thing, our "objectivity," be.

— Friedrich Nietzsche
On the Genealogy of Morals

Contents

PART ONE:

INNOCENCE

CHAPTER ONE: MICKY	1
CHAPTER TWO: DAVE	6
CHAPTER THREE: VIAGRA	11
CHAPTER FOUR: MICKY	15
CHAPTER FIVE: DAVE	19
CHAPTER SIX: VIAGRA	22
CHAPTER SEVEN: MICKY	26
CHAPTER EIGHT: RAVEN	30

PART TWO:

INTEGRITY

CHAPTER NINE: VIAGRA	39
CHAPTER TEN: VIAGRA	41
CHAPTER ELEVEN: VIOLET	45
CHAPTER TWELVE: DAVE	52
CHAPTER THIRTEEN: MICKY	55
CHAPTER FOURTEEN: VIOLET	59
CHAPTER FIFTEEN: DAVE	63
CHAPTER SIXTEEN: VIOLET	67
CHAPTER SEVENTEEN: MICKY	75
CHAPTER EIGHTEEN: RAVEN	77

PART THREE:

ESCAPE

CHAPTER NINETEEN: VIOLET	83

CHAPTER TWENTY: VIOLET   87
CHAPTER TWENTY-ONE: VIOLET   90
CHAPTER TWENTY-TWO: DAVE   95
CHAPTER TWENTY-THREE: MICKY   100
CHAPTER TWENTY-FOUR: VIOLET   103
CHAPTER TWENTY-FIVE: DAVE   107
CHAPTER TWENTY-SIX: VIOLET   111
CHAPTER TWENTY-SEVEN: MICKY   117

PART FOUR:

ABSOLUTION
CHAPTER TWENTY-NINE: MICKY   125
CHAPTER TWENTY-EIGHT: RAVEN   126
CHAPTER THIRTY: DAVE   127
CHAPTER THIRTY-ONE: VIOLET   129
CHAPTER THIRTY-TWO: MICKY   132
CHAPTER THIRTY-THREE: DAVE   137
CHAPTER THIRTY-FOUR: VIOLET   141
CHAPTER THIRTY-FIVE: DAVE   145
CHAPTER THIRTY-SIX: MICKY   148
CHAPTER THIRTY-SEVEN: VIOLET   151
CHAPTER THIRTY-EIGHT: MICKY   155
CHAPTER THIRTY-NINE: VIOLET   157
CHAPTER FORTY: MICKY   160
CHAPTER FORTY-ONE: DAVE   164
CHAPTER FORTY-TWO: VIOLET   166
CHAPTER FORTY-THREE: MICKY   169
CHAPTER FORTY-FOUR: VIOLET   171
CHAPTER FORTY-FIVE: DAVE   175
CHAPTER FORTY-SIX: VIOLET   180
CHAPTER FORTY-SEVEN: MICKY   185
ACKNOWLEDGEMENTS   191

PART ONE: INNOCENCE

CHAPTER ONE: MICKY

If you could discover the great secret of life and death, would you do it—even if it meant losing your mind? I've had very few fears in my life, but one of them has been that I'd lose it someday. Do most people worry about this kind of thing? I don't know; I don't know what most people worry about. Love, I guess, or when they're going to get married.

Or maybe they worry about finding a good job, because most people need to make money. And it's best if you do your duty and go to work. And when the weekend comes, you can go out and party and get drunk and laid and have a swell time.

But I don't work. And I don't play. I sit alone by myself and meditate. I contact, well...God. If you call it that. I contact something above or inside of myself.

Believe it or not, it's given me a strange ability: I'm able to read other people's minds. Not all the time, just sometimes, when I'm concentrating. I can know exactly what you're thinking and what the name of your cat is. Do you believe me? I could say I don't care if you believe me or not. But that wouldn't be true. I care more than you know. If you don't believe me, though, you could always go back to work—or play—or whatever you do to amuse yourself.

I'm amusing myself by typing on this computer.

It all began—or shall I say it all ended?—when I started reading this girl's mind, Viagra. (That was really her name, I'm not kidding.) I said, "Viagra, why are you thinking about having pork tonight when you know you'd rather have fish?"

And she said to me, "Micky!" (That's my name, Micky.) "What did you just say?"

"You heard me correctly, Viagra. And I'd rather have fish myself. I'm actually in the mood for white wine, which doesn't go as well with pork."

So that was that. We went to the fish market. We went to the liquor store. You see, Viagra and I had a cosmic understanding.

I don't have cosmic understandings with many people.

I am quite a loner type myself.

But with Viagra—not only did we get along incredibly in bed—our minds had a rare disease in common. You could call it madness. Let's just call it insanity. We were potentially insane.

That is, if you call the rest of the world sane.

Now I don't mean to give you the impression that I'm a flaming heterosexual or anything, because I'm not; I like guys too. But most people have to pigeonhole themselves into one sane category or another. It helps them to think they are sane. And I don't like to be sane, because I am *in*sane and I can read other people's minds to prove it.

It was late on a Tuesday night and I was sleeping over Viagra's. I was having an intense dream and everyone I knew was in it. Then what happened was this big red truck came directly at us and plowed us all down. We all got crushed and died. Now it's not true when they tell you that if you die in your dream it means you're dead. Not true at all. I've died many times in my dreams and I'm still alive. If you call this existence alive. I actually think I am quite dead to this world.

I know you won't believe me when I tell you what happened next with Viagra—but please remember that I told you we had a cosmic connection. By the way, I purposely haven't described her physically to you, the way so many stories do. Because first of all, this isn't a story, this is real life; and second of all, I find that totally boring. I mean, why can't you picture Viagra the way you want to picture her? What if I said she had hair as red as tomatoes on a summer night—then you'd never be able to get that image out of your head; whereas if I said her hair was as golden as the tip of a rocket, you would continue to think about her *that* way, wouldn't you?

The point I'm making is that I want you to picture Viagra with your own imagination. I don't want to spoil her with a falsely poetic description. I don't want to fake it with a pretty simile or metaphor. I'd rather have you do it yourself. I give you that much credit. I give you the power to have an imagination.

I was lying there with Viagra, finishing my dream—and I heard her start to scream; so I woke up from my dream and said, "V, honey, what's the matter?" And this is the part you won't believe: she proceeded to tell me the same dream about the red truck that I had just had.

Now Freud would take the meaning of a truck and the color red and turn it into some sexual innuendo; but I say when two people have the same dream at the same time, it is definitely worth noting.

We discussed it for about a half hour and returned to sleep in each other's arms. Ah, bliss. Those were the days.

The next morning, Viagra made bacon for breakfast, and since we weren't having white wine, I didn't care.

She patted me on the head and went off to her job. I never knew what she did. I wasn't interested. It was all the same to me. You wouldn't be interested either. You see, it doesn't make any difference:

Viagra went off to her job and there I was alone, ready for a thrilling day of my own creation. I went out on the street and saw all the people going to work. I bet you might like to know where we lived. Why should I tell you that? I told you, we have no particular hair color—or eye color—and I'll be damned if I tell you what city, town, or country we happen to reside in. So put us wherever you like. It's not going to change what happens in this story, this story about the secret meaning of life and death. Possibly my own death, possibly Sylvia's. I'm not going to tell you yet. Oh, sorry, I meant to say Viagra. Freudian slip. Sylvia was someone else, someone I don't remember, someone from a very long time ago.

Sylvia was my mother. And Seymour was my father. We grew up in a little town, but I'm not going to tell you where that was either. Invent it. Make it up. Use a little creativity.

It just so happens that Viagra looked very much like Sylvia, just as I looked very much like Seymour, which was only natural since I was his son.

But they both died. Guess how. Guess.

OK: get ready. They both got run over by a big red truck—as red as a big red tomato! How's that for a shock and surprise?

So that dream that I dreamed—I dreamed it a lot...and so did Viagra. You see, Viagra was really my sister. Well, half-sister. Her father was Garrick and he died in England. He drowned himself. He was a very intelligent man—or so I'm told. Viagra dreamed about him too sometimes. I never did.

So now you know. This is a story about the great mystery of life and death. Because any story about life is really a story about death. Isn't that where we're all headed? There are no real characters. There are no real situations. Life is full of illusion, like the color of people's hair. All you have to do is pretend what you like, pretend what you want, see it there before you and have it—in your mind. Have it there, have it now. Close your eyes—see it...now open your eyes: there it is!

See? I've taught you something, if you're not lazy. Refuse to be lazy. Refuse to be weak at all cost. See with your own eyes—not the eyes of everyone else at work. Please. For your own sake.

I thought I would skip to the end of this story, so when you get there you can look back with recognition and say, "Aha!" For by then, you will see it from a totally different perspective:

When Viagra returned from work that day, I said, "Let's go for a walk."

She asked, "Why?"

I said, "It's time."

So we walked down to the big boulevard—you know the one I mean—you can picture it with your own eyes, can't you? You can see it like one of those postcards of the *Champs Elysées*, can't you? With the headlights all one stream of white light and the taillights all one stream of red? Not like tomatoes, but like real rocket ships, rocket ships to nowhere.

4

And on the big boulevard, we waited and waited. Waited and waited. The waiting was interminable; it took forever. Yet it finally appeared. We saw it approaching in the distance: our big red truck. Our juicy, mouth-watering, ripe, red truck.

And I led her by the hand. I led her across the boulevard, where the red light turned into pure white light...and I touched her face and said, "Viagra, if there's anything or anyone I love in this world, it's you, my darling."

And we stood in the white light and awaited our oncoming big red truck....

Now you may wonder how I could be telling you this story—or where I could be telling it from. Or why I am telling it to you at all. I don't know the answers to these questions. I don't know what happened after that. I don't know where I am now and I don't know anything else—except that I know a lot more than you think.

It's just that I had nothing better to do today—that's really the truth. And if truth be told, as it so rarely is, I simply wanted to amuse myself—and you—with the true story of how I escaped from this world. This world of metaphors, similes, boulevards and rocket ships. Tomatoes and women with many different shades of hair.

And red toy trucks, big and powerful—as powerful as the imagination!—that lead us into a world where we can be free.

CHAPTER TWO: DAVE

When I'm driving, I'm free. You know the feeling? Do you drive? Maybe you drive, but probably not like me. I drive for a living. I'm a D.A. Delivery Associate. Don't let me hear you calling me a truck driver—I might smack you! I'm a D.A. and my home is the road. What's weird about me is that I drive and drive, but I have no idea what I deliver. Makes no difference to me. I just do my job. Which is to get from one place to another. It's not my business what's in back. I care about what's in front: the freedom of the road, moving forward.

Some of the happiest times I remember have been driving late at night. There was one night on I-95. It was the full moon—it was four A.M.—and they were playing Beethoven on the radio. Do you like Beethoven? He's OK, when you're in the mood. And he was perfect for that night at four A.M.

You have to realize, when you're driving by yourself, listening to music, blinking your lights at the other D.A.'s, there's a special feeling that you get, a feeling like your soul is ready to fly, like you could just fly and soar and gleam with happiness. Happiness without a reason, you know? Did you ever feel happiness without a reason? That's how I feel behind the wheel. Hey, sounds like a song:

That's how I feel

Behind the wheel

I like to sing and make up songs. But really, that's how I feel when I'm driving my truck. Oh yeah, my eighteen-wheeler. I feel like a giant, I feel like a stud. I *am* quite a stud if you want to know, actually. I've got pretty good muscles, nice tattoos, and a body to go with them that the women love. I really do feel good about myself—but not in a conceited way. Just in a free way. Like the great freeway! I'm sure that's been said before.

Anyway, I suppose you'd like to know, I have had my share of women. And yeah, I do enjoy the ladies. Occasionally, but don't spread it around, I've been known to be with a man, too. Sometimes at some of these rest areas, you can find a guy who wants to do you. What the hell? He enjoys it—and so do I, I must confess. I don't see anything wrong with pleasure shared with guys.

But I do prefer the ladies—and they prefer to be with me, I can tell you! But I can't think about them too much, you know. When I'm driving I've got to concentrate on the road. If I pay too much attention to my dick, I'd never reach my destination. There's this intersection of three highways in Jersey, Routes 1 and 9 and 22. When I was younger once I was jerking off in my truck as I was driving. I'll never forget that spot where I came, just as I was making the turn—and boy, we almost had a five-car pileup, I'll tell you! Jeez.

But that was a while ago, in my younger days. I'm still pretty young, in shape, feeling good. But I'm usually paying attention, getting to where I'm getting. It's a mystery to me what I'm delivering. I wouldn't want to know. I just deliver. Man, do I deliver! My job is to get it there. Think I'd be caught loading or unloading? Not me.

Anyway, I got a nice, shiny truck which I love like my mother. I am proud to be the driver of such a vehicle, such a power machine! I feel good about myself. Doesn't everyone? Isn't that how we're supposed to feel? Good about ourselves? Isn't that why God put us on this-here earth? To feel good about ourselves?

I don't understand some of these people you read about. They don't feel good about themselves, you know? Maybe they were brought up by their folks to feel fucked-up or something. But I just don't see the point. Why complain about life? If you just do what you're meant to do, there's no problem. I love life. I love being free on the road. Wouldn't trade it for any desk job in the world. No way.

So what can I tell you that would be interesting?

I'm just driving along at the moment, feeling pretty good. I'm listening to the radio. No Beethoven tonight—they're playing Pearl

7

Jam. I like that lead singer, forget his name. Heard an interview with him once—now that guy's got integrity. He sings about what he feels, what he believes in. He doesn't put up with the shit they try to throw his way. He does things *his* way. Man, I can respect that. If you can't do things your way, if you can't do what you believe in, then what's the point? Why should you do things other people's way? Can you imagine if they told me I had to drive a certain way? Or if they told me I couldn't smoke when I drive or something? I'd never do it. I'd quit. And I don't mean smoking. No sir. Either I'm free to be me...OK—another song, here goes:

Either I'm free

Free to be me

Aw, can't think of the rest. I'll leave it to Pearl Jam. They say it much better than I can: "I'm still alive." I like that. Yeah, I'm still alive and I do enjoy it. You know, a man's gotta feel good about who he is. Do you get what I'm saying? It's just easy. Why make it complicated?

I met this girl once. Oooo, she was nice. Prettiest girl I remember. One of the best times I ever had. She was real sweet, sensitive—and she knew just what I liked. She was a very caressing kind of girl. I met her at a country and western type bar on the road one night. She had hair that was like...I don't know. She had a smile that...oooo, it just got me. Right here. (I'm pointing to my heart.) I'd like to look her up sometime. I've got her number. Maybe I should call her. That would be nice.

Now she had one of those messed-up childhoods you hear about. Her father beat her when she was just a little girl. How can any daddy do something like that? I just can't imagine it. She was so sweet and little and pretty. How could her daddy beat her? Makes me want to cry, just thinking about it. You know, I cry and I'm a man. Not ashamed to admit it one single bit. When a man cries, it's a beautiful thing, you know. To be strong and able to cry, that's a good way to be.

Anyway, her daddy ended up killing himself. Years later. And serves him right too. How can anybody live with themselves after that? He drowned himself in a lake. Somewhere in England, I think. Can you imagine drowning? Must be awful. Can you imagine forcing yourself to do it? I can't imagine that at all. He must've had a messed-up childhood himself.

Life is pretty weird, you know? I guess I'm just lucky. I feel good. I'm always moving. I'm never bored. I feel like I can take a breath of fresh air, breathe it in…and breathe it out. Did you ever try that? If things get bad, just breathe it in and breathe it out. Like smoking. That's my philosophy of life.

Uh-oh. My beeper's going off. Must be my boss. Let me pull over to this gas station here. They've got a phone….

"Delivery."

"Hey, Shel, it's Dave."

"Dave! That was fast, man."

"Well, you lucked out for once. What's up? You got somethin' for me?"

"Yeah, I got somethin' you're really gonna like. Right near that girl you told me about."

"Which girl is that?"

"The one near 99, remember? You couldn't stop talking about her."

"Oh yeah, I was just thinking about her."

"Well, man, I'm givin you a night of love, if you want it—just take everything you got to the warehouse on 99—and then the night is yours."

"Hey, thanks, Shel, will do. You can count on me, Mr. Reliable, heh-heh."

"Night, Dave. Have fun, lover boy."

Well, golly gee. Like fate just planned it or something.

Uh-oh, another song's comin' on. I'll spare you my singing this time. I don't think I was really cut out for that. We're all cut out for something, and I don't think I was cut out for that. I was cut out for driving. I'm just a cut-out, a cardboard cut-out. That's a joke. I'm not serious. I'm just joking with you.

It's late. And I'm happy. I don't know when I've felt so happy. Hey, it's the full moon tonight again. Can you see it there, over to the right? I know you're not really here with me, but can you see it there? Almost kind of yellow? Reminds me of the night I heard that Beethoven. Let me switch the station, see what I can get....

Oh, I got something good here, don't know what it is. I never really know until they announce it. This one sounds pretty familiar, though. Oh, you know this one. They play it sometimes on the Fourth of July. It's got cannons shooting off in it. You know that one, don't you? It's real familiar.

Oh man, it's so nice, riding with the full moon, the almost yellow moon, and the music and cannons and weight of my truck behind me. Feeling strong, feeling powerful. Feeling like I'm pulling important stuff. Oh yeah, whatever I'm delivering, it must be important. Else why would I be doing it? Hah.

Yeah, I think I'll call that girl when I get done. I shouldn't be too far away from where she lives. Maybe we can hook up. Maybe we can have a date on the full moon. Maybe we can feel like a man and a girl ought to feel—good about ourselves, good about who we are, good about our lives, the moon, and the earth.

Yeah.

CHAPTER THREE: VIAGRA

It's the full moon and I feel so lonely. Do you mind if I talk to you? Sometimes the pain inside gets to be too much, especially on the full moon—and I need someone to talk to. You could sit beside me here by the window, and we can watch the moon together. It looks yellow tonight. I wonder why. I wonder what that means.

My name is Viagra. Now I know you'll laugh, but I swear my parents named me that before they invented the drug. It's really a pretty name, don't you think? If you forget about the drug connotations. And all the jokes—I'm so tired of all those jokes.

My brother Micky kids me about it too, but he does it in such an affectionate way. He really loves me—and I love him as well, more than anyone in the world. He has a tendency, though, to spin some yarns; so if you ever meet him, don't believe everything he says. He's got a great imagination, but sometimes I think he makes up some of his stories. That's OK; I know his heart is in the right place.

It's good to have a brother you can depend on. When our parents died, I didn't know how I could survive—and I might not have, if it hadn't been for Micky. He really took care of me then. But we were much younger. Now we're grown up, Micky's a little crazy—and I'm... well, I'm depressed right now. I'm lonely. I'm in despair over my life.

I have memories of my father beating me. I must have been about five. I remember trying to cover my naked body with my hands as he beat me with his belt—yet with all my screaming and crying, he kept thrashing and thrashing; and the one emotion I remember feeling was helpless indignation: How could you do this to me? What have I done to you? I am innocent! I remember thinking that I would hate him forever, that I would never forgive him; but the one person I have never forgiven has been myself. Whatever praise I receive as an adult, I always feel like damaged goods.

I don't hold out much hope for the therapists, the psychologists. What can they do for me now? I've had enough of them; I don't believe in them anymore. I've spent my life talking and analyzing and gestalting my pain away. I need something to release me from this dreary existence.

Why do most of us assume that another person in our lives will solve all our problems? I don't know why we do, but, to be very honest, most of us do. We're all longing for that special person we can share our lives with. But why, really? Isn't the whole concept a bit absurd at its root? It's what most of us want—yet it simply covers up the emptiness and loneliness inside each of us. Either we have the happy romance, the happy relationship, the happy marriage, or we live in a state of isolation and despair. This doesn't seem right somehow; isn't there another possibility?

Micky's father left him a lot of money, so he doesn't have to work. But we had different fathers. My father left me nothing...nothing but scars. Inner scars that have never gone away. Sometimes, on a good day, I think they've faded; but then they resurface—especially, it seems, on the full moon. I'm sensitive and I respond to the moon. I'm Pisces, a water sign, dreamy and emotional. Micky's Gemini—all mind—and sometimes two!

You know, there was one time that I met an extraordinary man. I've met lots of men, but I remember very few like him. He was probably just out for the sex, which I gave to him so tenderly. I don't really believe in soul mates, but if such a concept exists, perhaps he was one. I remember caressing every inch of his body, hoping I could reach his mind, his heart; and I didn't regret for one minute the time we spent together. But I doubt that I will ever see him again. It was just one of those magic-for-one-night experiences.

There was something about him, though—his sense of life? If I could have another chance, if I could see him again, perhaps he could heal some of the pain; perhaps he could cure me forever—who knows? I remember what it was like to have him inside me, deep, deep inside me. As if his power got to the very core of what hurt inside—and transformed it into pleasure, so that it didn't hurt anymore; and like a rain cloud that burst into the sun, it became a sun shower, or better yet, a rainbow.

Oh, sorry, I've been a little preoccupied with my thinking. We're supposed to be having a visit, watching the moon. The moon, they say, is a Great Goddess—and when the moon is full you can ask for a wish and the wish will come true. But they don't tell you that the Goddess will only grant your request if you truly believe in your wish. You have to believe in it as you ask for it.

The only problem is, I may believe in the Goddess, but I no longer believe in my wish. I have lost my hope for happiness. Trust me, it doesn't work in my life. I don't believe that happiness is possible for me. But let's not be overly sad or maudlin about it; I hate that. Let's be grateful for the things that do work out.

I'm lucky to have such a wonderful brother. He's always here for me. And I'm lucky to live in this house with this bay window and this view of the Moon Goddess. Shall we try to make a request? For old times' sake? Tell you what: you ask for whatever you most desire and I'll do the same. Remember, you're supposed to believe in it as you ask. I'll try my best, I really will.

OK. Let's try. Let's believe....

The doorbell's ringing. Who could be ringing my bell on the full moon? Oh, I can see who it is through the front window. It's Mrs. Llop, my crazy neighbor. I wonder what she wants this time. I'm opening the door:

"Hello, Mrs. Llop, how are you tonight?"

"Good evening, Viagra, if it *is* a good evening. I need to talk to you about something."

"Would you like to come in?"

"That won't be necessary, dear. It's about my station wagon, Maggie."

"Oh, Maggie. How is Maggie doing?"

"Not very well tonight, I'm afraid. I know I've asked you this before, but I need to ask you again. Please don't park your white car near Maggie. I can't get her started, and I know it's because your car has been saying insulting things to my Maggie and hurting her feelings again."

"Mrs. Llop, I'm really sorry about this. I forgot. I was in a hurry earlier and parked my car on the street. Let me move it now. It won't happen again."

"I hope not. I can't function if Maggie doesn't function. She's very sensitive, you know. And very touchy when she's teased for being a station wagon."

"I understand. Let me do it now."

"Thank you, Viagra. Good night."

Try not to judge my neighbor. We're all entitled to our idiosyncrasies, especially on the full moon. Let me move my car. I'll be right back....

OK. I've put my car in the garage and I'm back at my window.

Are you still there? What time is it? God, it's nearly midnight. It's good of you to have stayed with me all this while. And now it's the witching hour, midnight on the full moon. What magic could possibly be in store? She is at her highest height now—she looks promising, don't you think? Is she smiling or is it just my imagination? Does the imagination tell us what is true?

I feel like something is about to happen. I feel so scared suddenly. Where are you? Are you still there? I feel completely alone now. Even you have left me alone. I feel like something terrible is about to happen. I can't explain it. I'm going to scream.

Ahhhh! The phone is ringing! Who could be calling me now? No one calls me this late. Hardly anyone calls me at all. I'm afraid to answer it. But it keeps ringing. It sounds sweet almost, as if it has love in it. Love somewhere in the ringing. Could it be what I'm thinking?

Let me find out. I'd better get it before he hangs up. I know who it is. I'm sure of it. Thank you, Goddess. Great Goddess of the full moon.

CHAPTER FOUR: MICKY

It was the full moon and I couldn't sleep. So at around 2 A.M., I decided to go for a ride with Raven, my black Camaro. Raven and I had a special connection—that is, for a man and his car. I could tell you stories that you wouldn't believe. Like how Raven reacted to my former girlfriend. I kid you not, every time she got into the car, Raven broke down. He was jealous of my girlfriend. Raven was a queer car. But you'll never believe this.

Raven used to speak to me in other ways, too. For instance, there was no clock inside—I swear—only a radio. But sometimes the time would mysteriously appear. You know, instead of saying a radio station like 102.7, it would suddenly say 1:08, with the colon blinking and everything. I discovered that Raven was communicating to me in a secret code. My challenge was to decipher the code. But the night he said 1:08, it was easy. I was hunting around for a parking space for over an hour. Guess what time I actually found the space: you guessed it. Exactly 1:08.

Now in case I need to say it again, these are all true stories I'm telling you. Do you think I would invent this stuff out of thin air?

I was riding with Raven at around 2 A.M. on the night of the full moon. Raven was happy because I no longer had this girlfriend and he was humming along at a merry pace.

"Where shall we drive tonight, Rave?" I asked.

"Whrrrr," said Raven.

"Whrr, as in, 'were?' Let's go there, boy."

So the two of us drove, as it were, to wherever we were.

And where were we? Suddenly I knew. I had no recollection of driving there. We were on Viagra's street.

"Look where we are, Raven. I don't know where we *were*, but I do know where we *are*."

And I decided to drive by and see if Viagra's light was still on, knowing that she didn't usually keep late hours.

Well, when I got to the front of her house, I did see lights on; but I also saw a red tractor-trailer parked in the street. And I thought, uh-oh, Viagra is celebrating tonight—and good for her. My sister seemed to have a thing for truck drivers.

So I wondered, What shall I do? Am I up for a little mischief? I turned off the headlights, parked Raven in the driveway, got out and tiptoed up to the window.

And what should I see in the window? It was a breathtaking sight to behold. I saw a beautiful woman with long, iridescent hair—and I saw one of the hunkiest guys I had ever seen in my life. What an ass on this guy! They were both naked on the sofa—and he was doing it with my sister. Well, I just had to laugh. I was happy for my sister. She certainly could have used a good time. But what about me? Should I hide in the bushes like a sick peeping Tom? Or should I head back to Raven and get the hell out of there?

What do you think I did, knowing me as well as you think you do at this moment in time? Did I play the respectful brother? Or did I try to create some drama, so that I'd have a good story to tell you?

I'll let you contemplate this for thirty seconds....

The first possibility is that I turned around, went back to Raven, and drove home like a good, little boy. Do you really think I did that? Had I done that, this chapter would be finished right now. But if you look ahead, you will see that there are several more pages. So I must have done something other than go home.

Raven kept watch and—who knew?—maybe he'd get something going with that red-hot tractor-trailer when I was out of sight.

I watched for a while through the front window. The moonlight shone through the back bay window in such a way that you'd think a film crew took hours to set up the shot. It lit parts of them from behind, so that their shadows and curves were illuminated in the most erotic

16

poses; and I couldn't decide who I desired more: my sister or the man she was with.

I love taboos. I love what's forbidden. I love to rebel against society. These days, being with a man is no big deal; but our society still doesn't accept being with your sister—or half-sister. Viagra would probably never admit it, but we experienced a little of that during our Cape Cod summer together—and I assure you, it was a very beautiful experience. What could be wrong with anything you might want to do with another person, as long as that person is willing? And we were both willing to experience that kind of love together. I wasn't at all ashamed of it; and I hoped we would try it again in the future, which we eventually did, as I've told you.

As I watched the two of them going at it on the living room couch, with the MGM lighting and the full moon borrowed by Scenic Artists, USA—oh, sorry, I just gave away the country, as if you hadn't guessed it by now—I started to get a little bit aroused. And the thought crossed my mind of taking it out right there and joining in with them from a distance; but the idea finally creeped me out. I decided I'd feel just a little too pervy to permit myself doing something like that.

I turned around to check on Raven, and it seemed like he was developing a nice relationship with the tractor-trailer. So knowing that he was out of harm's way, I decided to pursue my escapade just a little further. I tiptoed around to the side door, which I knew was always unlocked, and I slipped into the laundry room and crept slowly in the dark toward the living room.

I could hear the long, slow panting of ecstasy close by. I wanted to join this ecstasy; I wanted to be a part of it myself. I longed to be with my sister again, but I also longed to check out this new man. I slowly undressed myself back in the laundry room. My body was not that bad. Not like the truck driver's, but still, nothing to scoff at.

At first I folded my clothes on the floor, but realized that I might as well wash them while I was there, so I put them in the washing machine for later, as I figured I'd be staying the night. Then, naked and aroused, I crawled my way slowly down the hallway toward the living room.

17

Everything was very still, very quiet, except for the slow-motion sound of their ecstatic sighs, their happy breathing, and the occasional "Ah" or "Oh, Dave." I assumed that this was his name.

I drew closer to the living room; I drew closer to their sound. I could feel myself a part of them—I was completely turned on. I didn't know if I could stand it any longer. I wanted to merge with them. I heard them starting to come—they were nearly screaming; my sister sounded like she was in heaven, as if she were singing. And he sounded masculine and guttural, like he was singing himself in a deep, powerful way. And they came together—and so did I. I couldn't contain myself.

I lay there in the hallway close to the living room. I felt so high from the excitement. When you do something truly dangerous, it's an exhilarating feeling, like you've rebelled against the rules and have gotten away with it big time. I was delirious with joy.

But with the depletion of my energy and the ensuing exhaustion setting in, I changed my plans, decided not to join them, and headed back to the laundry room. I retrieved my clothes, got dressed, headed out the side door and entered Raven as quickly and quietly as I could. It seemed like he had said goodnight to the truck and was more than ready to go.

I turned the ignition, but as I did, I noticed my red Flair pen and paper lying on the front seat—and I suddenly got a crazy idea. I started writing:

Please call me at your earliest convenience. It is very important that I talk to you about my sister, Viagra. You can reach me any time of the day or night. It is urgent that you call me. Thank you, Micky.

I wrote down my phone number below that, opened Raven's door and quietly walked over to the big truck. I placed my note in an obvious place under the windshield wiper—I had to climb up to do it—and headed back to Raven.

We pulled away slowly at first and then we sped down the highway on what was by then, a dark, moonless night.

CHAPTER FIVE: DAVE

After the moon set, I covered her up with a blue blanket.

"Dave?" she mumbled, half asleep.

"Oh sorry, baby, just wanted to tuck you in. Everything all right with you?"

"Mmm...better than all right. Are you staying over?"

"Yeah, I'll stay for a little while. But I've got to hit the road when it gets light. You're beautiful, you know that?"

"Well, I feel beautiful with you," she said.

We cuddled up together under the blanket. God, I felt like I really loved this girl! What was it about her? Why did she have that effect on me? That mysterious effect on me?

She was like a sorceress and I was helpless under her spell. She made me sensitive and made me feel like a poet, like I could write great poetry—even better than my songs!

What is it about a certain kind of woman that does this to a man? What mysterious force is at work? We certainly had a connection, I'll tell you. I was never really the settling down kind, but if I ever met someone that I could settle down with, it would be her, I thought that night.

We cuddled in each other's arms and drifted into sleep. Is there any better feeling in the world? To drift into sleep with your enchantress? To give yourself over to the spell of love?

Yeah, I really did feel like I loved her as I lay there, falling asleep, dreaming of green grass, miles of green grass. We were running, the two of us, Viagra and me...we were running on the green grass...we were naked...we were very young, like teenagers, each of us, running on this green grass that went on forever.

The breeze blew over us and lifted us high...and we floated up to the clouds, laughing like kids; in fact, we *were* kids—no longer teenagers—we became kids again and we were playing in the clouds. Everything was perfect. Everything was innocent. Everything was free. What a great world!

But suddenly this bad cloud started coming our way. It was a dark, bad cloud. All the other clouds got scared. And we all started flying away as fast as we could from this one bad cloud that was getting closer and closer. It really was scary, I'll tell you.

Then little Viagra in the dream started screaming. I took her hand like a big brother and told her everything was going to be all right. But she kept screaming.

And then I woke up—and Viagra really *was* screaming. I whispered, "Hey...hey, what's the matter, baby? Were you having a bad dream?"

"Oh...Dave, yes I was. I was having this dream. I have this same dream over and over."

"Well, you're OK now, baby. I was having a scary dream, too. But see, we're both here and we're both OK. And I love you, Viagra."

I couldn't believe I said that, but I meant it. I really did.

It was a very tender moment there together, the two of us under the blue blanket. We must have drifted off after that, because I don't remember anything else until we woke up the next morning.

Man, did that woman know how to make a good cup of coffee.

"This tastes almost as good as Dunkin' Donuts," I said.

"We aim to please," she smiled, looking like my dream girl, even in the morning.

"You want to walk me out to my truck?" I smiled back.

"Sure," she said, trying not to look sad.

I reached over and kissed her pretty lips, hoping that it wouldn't be too long before the next time I saw her. We kissed for a long while, considering that I knew I was due back soon.

We didn't say much of anything as we walked down the path from her house to the street. The sun was beginning to rise over the houses across the way, promising me a golden day of driving on the highway.

When we got to my truck, I really didn't know what to say to her—so we both kind of gazed at each other—and I tried to make light of the moment, giving her a good grin, because I could tell it was hard for her to say goodbye to me.

"Hey—looks like there's something under my wiper there. You want to climb up and get it for me?"

"Sure," she said.

"Here, let me give you a boost."

And she climbed up the side steps like a real pro, reached for the piece of paper, looked like she was about to read it but then thought better of it, like she suspected it might be personal or something, and handed it to me.

"What is it?" she asked.

"I don't know," I said, glancing at the red writing. Right away I saw the words, "my sister, Viagra," and "urgent" and "Micky." I didn't know she had a brother—and something told me this might be a private note, something I shouldn't tell her about yet.

"Oh, just a kid's prank, I think," I chuckled as I stuffed the note in my back pocket. "I hope to see you again, Viagra—next time I'm up this way."

"I'll look forward to that," she said with a gleam in her eye. "You made me feel so good last night."

"I feel the same way. You take care now."

"Bye-bye, Dave."

And I hopped up on my driver's seat and gave her a loud honk. She kind of jumped and we both laughed as I buckled up and started the engine. Then we waved goodbye and I drove off in the direction of the rising sun.

CHAPTER SIX: VIAGRA

What is this thing about beauty? Would Dave really care for me if I weren't considered beautiful? How would I feel about him if he weren't a hot guy? Even when they make movies about real people, they always get glamorous movie stars to play the roles—and they're always better looking than the real-life characters. Why can't they have a love story with average-looking people?

It makes me wonder how real my happiness is. Because I surely feel, or think I feel, happier than I can remember for a long time. But how, for instance, would Dave feel about me if I were mediocre looking? Would he feel anything for me at all? Does my personality—who I am—have anything to do with it? Does he really love me, Viagra—or this fantasy woman of his?

Because I guess deep down, below the surface, I don't have much self-worth or self-esteem; so it's natural to question Dave's true feelings for me. Still, haven't women tried for centuries to make themselves look beautiful? The men have to make themselves rich for the women; and the women have to make themselves beautiful for the men. What kind of world is this?

Certainly not a world that I choose to participate in. Maybe that's why I've been lonely. I've refused to play the game. The love and marriage game. But if you don't play by the rules of the game, doesn't it mean that you lose? I hope not. I don't choose to play this game. I've decided that if I continue to see Dave, I will continue to be myself, whatever self I choose to be, beautiful or ravishingly ugly if I feel like it.

Earlier today I fantasized that it might be funny to look hideous the next time I see him—my hair in curlers, cream on my face—something like that, just as an experiment, to see how he'd react. But I don't know that I'd really have the guts to go through with it. How many women would? We all want to look gorgeous for our men. And we spend hours trying our best to do just that.

But I'm not interested in painting my eyes, my nails, my toenails; I'd rather paint a painting. In fact, I used to paint when I was younger. I don't really know why I stopped. All my teachers said I had talent. I guess it was the lack of encouragement that our society gives to the artist: we should do something practical with our lives.

But after Dave left, so early this morning, I decided that I should resume my artwork, and try to apply to the canvas what most women apply to their faces. Let the beauty manifest itself outwardly, from an inner expression—rather than an outer superficiality expressing itself on the surface, if that makes any sense. Now I sound like Micky: always the double Gemini personality.

Dave is Sagittarius, one of my favorite signs. And one of the sexiest, too. I was glad to find that out. I don't know why intelligent people pooh-pooh astrology. It's been respected by kings and queens and presidents throughout history. And though I don't rule my life by it, it's always fascinated me; and there seems to be some truth in it.

But then, as a Pisces, I'm something of a mystic. Well, in a way, so is Micky. He claims to read minds occasionally. He has actually wowed me a few times, telling me exactly what I've been thinking. He says that this power comes from his meditations, which he usually does late at night. I'm in awe of him. I know that he writes a lot, and I hope he eventually does something with his writing. I think he's got some unusual ideas.

But I'm going off on tangents—and what's really on my mind is Dave and the wonderful time we had together. I'd love to tell someone about it. Who can I call? I could call Ann, the woman I volunteer with once a week at the hospital; or I could call Frieda from work; but no, they wouldn't really be happy for me. Why don't I call Micky and see what he says?

It's ringing....

"You have unfortunately reached my phone machine. This is Micky, in case you haven't guessed. Please leave a message and perhaps I will return your call if I have the inclination. Thank you."

"Oh, Micky, I'm sorry you're not there. This is Viagra. Remember me? I've got some good..."

"Viagra! Hi honey!"

"Oh, Micky, I'm so glad you're there."

"Yeah, I was just finishing a meditation."

"Oh, sorry to interrupt."

"No, really, I was just taking my last few breaths. Now let me guess why you're calling."

"OK."

"You've met a man."

"Yes; well, that's not hard to figure out."

"His name is...let me see...Dave."

"Wow. You must really be in touch after your meditation!"

"He drives a big, red tractor-trailer."

"Oh, come on, Micky. How do you do this?"

"Viagra, I cannot tell a lie. You had the best sex you've had for a long time."

"You are really something. How did you know? I don't have to tell you *anything*."

"OK. I can't continue this. I was driving by last night. I was there."

"You *what*?"

"I was driving by and saw the truck, so I walked up to the house and saw the two of you through the window. It was really hot, V!"

"I can't believe you saw us! So what did you do then?"

"Uh, I left. What else could I do? Join the two of you uninvited? Ha-ha."

"I can't believe you saw us."

"I saw it all."

"So what did you think?"

"Not bad, V. Not bad at all. Your taste is improving."

"Well, this guy—he's really sensitive and caring; we met once before. And I think we'll be seeing each other again. It feels like it's something real, you know?"

"I hope so for your sake, honey. I really do. It would be great for you to have a man."

"I feel so happy. Happier than I've felt in a long time. But I don't know whether I can trust it. Happiness is such an illusive thing, you know?"

"Oh listen, I got a beep...just a second...."

...Hmmm...I'm waiting here at my window for a long time. It isn't like Micky to keep me waiting; it must be important. Wait a minute...how did he know Dave's name?

"Sorry, V, this is an important call and I should take it."

"Oh, OK, is everything all right?"

"Yeah, fine. Talk to you soon?"

"Sure."

"Bye."

That was strange. He had a very strange tone in his voice. Oh well, I'm not going to get frazzled by it; it was probably one of his crazy friends. He's always getting involved in complicated situations.

It's starting to get dark and I need to think about dinner. How about a glass of wine to celebrate? Let me put on some music, have some wine, and try to enjoy this feeling of new love. Could it really be? Finally?

I refuse to take this seriously. Famous last words! But oh, Dave...if you could be here...if you could be a part of my life...would I be happy then? Would I finally have some happiness?

I guess I'll have to wait and find out. Let's see what they're playing. Ah, Brahms. I know it. Third symphony, third movement. That haunting theme they used for some Hitchcock movie, I think.

Well here I am, sitting at my window, looking out at the trees, drinking my wine and watching it get dark. It certainly feels like a Hitchcock movie—or some movie—contemplating the fate of my new, haunting, ever-so-illusive love.

CHAPTER SEVEN: MICKY

I love the sound of my sister's voice. From as early as I can remember, it was always my sister's voice that soothed me. When her father came to visit us on Sundays and threatened to whack me if I misbehaved, it was always the sound of Viagra's tender words that calmed me down.

I was in the middle of a deep meditation. People don't realize what it's like to be in touch with a realm that is higher, yet at the same time, within oneself. Some nights I feel like I make a new kind of progress, like I'm really able to block out the world—and also my neurotic (if not psychotic) mind—and achieve a balance of forces within and without, above and below me.

When the phone rang, which I heard somewhere in the distance, hardly disturbing the new plateau I had found, I realized I had forgotten to turn off the volume; so it was my sister's voice that brought me back to reality; and I decided to answer since I hadn't spoken to her in a while.

"Hi. It's Micky. Please leave a message after the tone. I appreciate it. Thanks."

"Micky, it's Viagra. Are you there?"

"Hello...."

"Oh hi, Micky, I'm glad you picked up."

"Viagra, it's good to hear your voice, how are you?"

"I'm really good, I think."

"Oh, good.... You'll have to excuse me; I'm a little spaced. I just had a great meditation. But I heard your voice up there in the clouds and decided to come down where the phone was."

"Oh, sorry to interrupt."

"No, really, I was just taking my last few breaths. Let me guess why you're calling."

"OK."

"You've met an incredibly sexy guy."

"Yes, but that's not so hard to figure out."

"You had the best sex you've had in a long time."

"Well, that's logical. What else?"

"Hmm...his name is...Dave."

"Wow!"

"And he drives a big, red, tractor-trailer."

"You are incredible! Did you know this somehow? You ought to go on TV!"

"Naaaah, it always looks so fake on TV."

"You're right."

"So you're feeling happy? Do you think you'll see him again?"

"I think we will; he says we will. We had a wonderful time together. And I do feel happy. Happier than I've felt in a long time. But I don't know whether I can trust it. Happiness is such an illusion, you know?"

At that moment I got a call-waiting. "V, hold on a sec...I got a beep."

"OK."

"Hello?"

"Hello, is this Micky?" The voice sounded slightly southern, as sexy as I expected.

"Yes it is...who is this?"

"Uh, my name is Dave and you left a note on my truck."

"Oh, hi. I'm glad you called. Where are you calling from?"

"I'm a few hours away from you. You live near your sister?"

"Yeah."

"Listen, was that some kind of joke? It's gotten me really worried."

"No, sorry, no joke at all. Um...can I call you back? I'm on the other line."

"No, that's impossible. I'm at a pay phone."

"Oh, OK. Let me get off. I'll be right back."

"Right."

"V?"

"Yes?"

"I'm sorry. This is an important call and I should take it."

"Oh, OK, is everything all right?"

"Yeah, fine. Talk to you soon?"

"Sure."

"Bye, Viagra."

"Bye."

"Dave?"

"Yeah?"

"Hi. I'm back."

"Now listen, man. You really got me worried. I care for your sister. And I wish you didn't go leaving notes on a guy's truck, you know? Your sister almost saw it. And it was really hard to act cool about it. So what's so important that you want to talk to me about?"

"Forgive me, Dave, but I didn't know how else to get in touch with you. I happened to be driving by last night and saw that you were there. I've got nothing against you seeing my sister, by the way; so don't worry about that."

"Well, then what's the problem?"

"I don't think it's something we can get into over the phone."

"Listen, man, I want you to tell me what's going on—and I want you to tell me now."

"Dave, I'm sorry...it's not something I'm really permitted to talk about...and we'll have to arrange a time and place to meet...if you really care about my sister."

"Christ...look, I'm pretty far away and I don't know how soon I'll be back. And when I do come back I want to spend the time with Viagra."

"Well, maybe we can meet somewhere in between? You're two hours away, you say?"

"Yeah, about that."

"Well, let's pick a spot—you know the places on the road better than me. Pick a spot and I'll meet you there."

"Man, this is silly. Why can't you just tell me about it now?"

"Dave, sir, with all due respect, a matter of this urgency should not be dealt with over the phone. I'm not very good on the phone, see—and

I need to look you in the eye when I say what I need to say to you. Does that make sense?"

"I suppose."

"Good."

"So when do you want to meet?"

"The sooner the better. Pick a spot on the highway, if you like."

"All right. There's this truck stop with a rest area and some picnic tables about an hour south of you on Route 99. I'll be headed up that way tonight. Can you do it tonight? Can I meet you there tonight?"

"No problem. What time?"

"How about 1:30? Let's make it two to be safe. Are you a night person?"

"Definitely."

"Good. Then I'll meet you there at two. It's just after the fork in the road. Stay on 99. You better be there, man. I'll wait fifteen minutes."

"Oh, I'll definitely be there. You can count on it."

"Good. Later."

"Bye, Dave, you won't regr..." But he had already hung up.

Excitement coursed through my veins. I threw off my clothes and got into the shower. I made the water as hot as I could stand it. The steam filled the room and burned away any fear I had. I turned the hot water into the iciest cold I could bear and stood there, like being naked under a waterfall, and let the freezing cascade purge my soul. I was a new man. I was more alive than ever before.

I got dressed, got my keys, and headed out to Raven. I needed time to gas up and go to the car wash. Raven had to shine. Raven had to gleam in the night. I was ready to mount Raven and drive southward on Route 99 toward a destination that was destined to be...my destiny.

CHAPTER EIGHT: RAVEN

OK. There's something that you need to understand right away, before I go any further. We cars and trucks and vehicles have a certain ethic amongst ourselves. We call it Proper Vehicular Behavior or PVB. In our world, it is considered the greatest breach of etiquette to go against these principles of integrity. And first and foremost on the list is loyalty to one's master, one's owner, or, as set forth in the official *Manual of Ethics*, one's driver.

It is my duty to explain these principles to you before I go any further with my story, so that you will understand the outrage I felt toward that...monster...the night of the full moon in Viagra's driveway. At first I thought it would be pleasant to have a nice visit with a vehicle from another class, a class that most of my fellow sports cars look down upon. But I'm not that way. I have received from my master, Micky, the highest regard for all classes of people, animals, and vehicles.

But now I understand why this elitism prevails among my peers, as I experienced first-hand the vulgarity of the lower vehicles.

At first I thought it amusing to be conversing with this sort of uneducated, highway type; and I was more than willing to learn from the experience—and perhaps, to even have a few laughs. But apparently, they do not teach these vehicles any sort of proper manners or appropriate behavior for conversing with members of a higher class.

I didn't mind so much that this red, vulgar monstrosity was trying to make the moves on me; I rather expected this and found it quite touching actually. But when she tried to reveal—and get me to actually *see*—the contents of what was hidden inside her *derrière*, I had to firmly bring the conversation to a halt. You see, this is just not done. I was profoundly appalled. First and foremost, we are loyal to our masters—

and never, without exception, do we ever reveal the private contents of our masters' belongings in any part of our vehicles: front seat, glove compartment, back seat or trunk. It is considered the highest breach of loyalty and etiquette.

Do you think I would ever reveal to another vehicle the contents of *my* trunk? I would rather have my carburetor replaced (and believe me, it is a very painful procedure) than tell any other vehicle such a thing. But this is just what the truck was trying to do, perhaps as a ploy to cozy up to me.

I had to say, "Stop it! Stop it! I'm going to put wax in my gears! I'm not interested in what lies inside your long behind—so stop telling me how important it is."

We spent the rest of our visit in silence; and every time she made another attempt, I just ignored it. Thank the God of Junkyards that she never actually revealed it. I would have been mortified, just mortified. This is how I was brought up.

Now the reason why I'm telling you this is because, after such a beautiful drive with my master Micky, whom I love and respect and adore, we pulled into this parking lot type of place—and who should be there but this vulgar monstrosity whose name I will never repeat to you. And it was my cruel fate that night—in fact, two nights in a row— to have to sit next to her again and bear her improprieties and lack of education.

I decided that the best way to deal with the situation was with total silence, which is just what I did. Not a word to that mongrel.

Instead, I focused my attention on the two men standing between us, Micky and the driver of the cretin, who seemed like a perfect gentleman to me. Let me explain to you how our car-senses work, as you probably have no knowledge of them. We can see everything in front of us, but we cannot hear it; and conversely, we can hear everything that goes on inside us, but we cannot see it.

So at first I observed Micky approaching the gentleman man, a very handsome fellow indeed, and just the sort I'd had in mind for my master, after he finally dropped that whore of a girl he'd been seeing. I simply refused to drive her anywhere; I simply refused. She was extremely vulgar too; a human version of our brazen friend over there.

By the way, do you prefer hearing this account in the past or the present? We vehicles are very versatile with such things, as we can't quite comprehend the concept of tense; and past, present and future are all one to us. But I believe I've heard it said that humans need to be there in the moment or some such hogwash, so let me tell you this account as if you were actually there and watching it through my headlights.

Micky, with his adorable curly hair, is going over and shaking hands with the handsome man. They're looking very serious. The handsome man doesn't look happy at all. He almost looks like he could start a fight with Micky. But Micky is doing a lot of talking; he seems to be explaining something. The handsome man is listening. And now what's happening is very strange: it almost looks like the handsome man is ready to punch Micky; but instead he starts to cry. It's a very tender sight, this sturdy, strong man starting to cry. He quickly stops himself, though, and reaches for his red handkerchief in his back, left pocket.

Right now they don't seem to be saying anything, and Micky is gently patting him on the back. They're coming toward me. I'm ready. They're coming my way. I think they're coming inside. I'm very glad. I would very much like to offer a seat or a ride to this man. And I would love for us all to drive away and leave that vulgar vehicle alone by itself.

The doors are opening and now I can hear:

"Have a seat. Here, I'll put on some music. What do you like?"

"All sorts of stuff, thanks. But I really don't need music now. I'm just trying to get together what you told me. It's a little bit of a shock."

"Well, I thought it was important that you knew."

"Yeah, I guess I'm glad that you told me. I don't really know what to do about it, though."

"Think it through and make the right decision. I just thought you should be informed."

"Well, thanks, I'm a little blown away."

"It's OK. That's perfectly natural. Would you like a beer? I've got some in my cooler here."

"Sure, that'd be great."

Micky is getting the beer and turns on my radio.

"Here you are, sir. Something seems to be wrong with my radio. I've put on the rock station but can only get classical. Hope that's all right."

I have been manipulating the circuitry of my radio, which I'll tell you more about later. I want to set a certain kind of mood.

"Oh, fine, I like classical," says the man.

"Do you? Well, do you know what this is? I can't believe they're playing this."

"Sounds familiar."

"Really?"

"Not sure."

"It's a work by Menotti about the Children's Crusades. I know it because I sang in the children's chorus when I was a boy—I got to be in it once. It was one of the highlights of my childhood."

"Sounds like a great experience."

"Oh, it was. And when I hear it as an adult, I realize how deep it is. But it's very obscure; they hardly ever play it. It's very sad too, about a bishop who gave the children permission to go on the Crusade—and then they all drowned. But he still hears their voices. I cry every time I hear it."

"I guess we both cry, then."

"Yeah, but I'm never ashamed of my tears. I'm never ashamed of anything I choose to do."

Micky sounds really intense when he says this. And now there is a long silence. I think I can hear the sound of someone's hand sliding across someone's clothes. It's a nice, massaging kind of sound.

The handsome man says, "Ahhhh."

And Micky says, "Yeah, you just need to relax."

And I hear the sound of a zipper being unzipped...and the handsome man says a longer "Ahhhhhh." I love it when people feel good together on my seats.

The handsome man is starting to breathe harder...and now he's starting to moan; but I know from past experience with Micky that it's a

33

good kind of moaning—not a painful kind at all. And now he says, "Oh, man, oh, man"—and he's yelling a little, nice yelling—loud....

Everything has gotten very quiet suddenly.

Finally, Micky says, "Thank you, sir."

And the man says, "No, thank *you*, sir!"

And now they're laughing together.

After a few moments, Micky asks, "Who are you, Dave? The man who comes out of the sky to save our souls?" So that's his name, Dave. A good name.

"Who am I?" he laughs. "I'm just a guy who likes to make people feel good. If I can make someone feel good, if I can make someone happy, then I'm happy."

"What a philosophy!"

"Yeah, well, it's a philosophy that works pretty good for me."

"Oh, it works pretty good for me, too," says my master. I can tell he is smiling.

"Listen," says Dave, "I've been driving all day and I need to get some shut-eye. Next time I'm up your way, I'll give you a buzz."

"That'd be great; I'll look forward to that."

And they open my doors and get out. They're shaking hands in a very macho, masculine way...and now Micky is coming back inside and starting me up.

"Raven!" he shouts. "Let's go home, boy!"

And he presses my pedal down real hard and strong all the way back on Route 99.

The first light is starting to rise out of the east as I sit in our driveway, awaiting the new day. I'm preparing a special treat for my master when he wakes up. I've only done it a few times, but I know he loves it. It's a chance for us to communicate together. They never put a clock inside me, but luckily a tiny computer chip fell in when I was on the assembly line, which enables me to show the time when I so desire. And I'm making the radio say 2:38, the time when the high peak of happiness between Micky and Dave seemed to occur.

34

I hope that when Micky sees 2:38, he'll remember that time of great joy, because I love Micky and want him to be happy. I know that too often he has a troubled soul. And I care for him in the deepest way a car can care for his master. OK, 2:38 it is. Done.

It's getting brighter now; and the dawning sunlight is making a nice reflection on my shiny, black hood. As the sun comes up and I wait here in the driveway for my master to take us on our first exciting ride of the day, I must confess, in spite of my previous antagonism, that I can't help but wonder: What could be hidden in the back of that big red truck? What is back there that could possibly be so important?

What could it be?

I wonder.

PART TWO: INTEGRITY

CHAPTER NINE: VIAGRA

It's been two weeks and I haven't heard from Dave. I thought he would have called me by now. If he had a cell phone, I would have called him— but he doesn't have one; I guess he's too free-spirited for that.

I've been feeling depressed again. It seems like whenever there's hope for anything, that hope gets destroyed. I had a taste of something beautiful with him; but now that beauty feels like an empty fantasy, like a happy dream at best.

Yet I refuse to make another suicide attempt. I tried it once and ended up in the hospital nearly dead—and it was worse than death. I never want to go through that again.

So I've made a decision. I've had this in the back of my mind for a long time. I am going to leave the life that I know—at least for a while.

A few years ago, I knew a dynamic yet sensitive man. His name was Hans, from Germany, and we worked together briefly. But he left his job to start an artists' colony with his wife, Erda. He knew I was unhappy, and being the kind man that he was, assured me that I would always have a home there if I so desired.

His mission, he said, was to create a society of artists, those who chose to leave their worlds behind them for one reason or another. And anyone was welcome—except for one stipulation: you had to leave your life behind and devote yourself to your work, your art, whatever form it might take.

In the past few days, as I realized that Dave would not be calling me and I felt my depression return with this realization, I've decided that my only alternative is to join Hans and Erda. I hear they've created a special place; and after several years now, it appears to be blossoming with success. Frieda is in touch with Hans and tells me that the artists are in awe of him, that they'll do anything he says, anything for the sake of art. She thinks it might be some sort of cult. I hope I'm not getting into anything dangerous.

Still, it is what I must do. I can resume my painting there. I can leave this life behind me. I have nearly made my decision and have already given my notice at work. I'm going to wait three more days to be sure. If I don't hear from Dave by then—and I really don't expect to at this point—I will gather my things and go.

I called Hans yesterday and he was delighted to hear from me. He said they've developed quite a society there—but that it's a secret one, and I am never to reveal its whereabouts or members. I promised him that I wouldn't. He said there were now several stipulations for living there: one, to make a complete break with everyone you know, your entire life as you know it; two, to tell no one where you are going; and three, to commit yourself to your new life for at least one month.

I told him I had no problem with these stipulations and that I'd give him my answer in three days. I know I'm going to do it, though. I somehow know I will not hear from Dave.

I don't mean to give any man such power over me; but when you meet someone you think you can love—and when that love, for whatever reason, seems impossible or ill-fated—and when this seems to be your continual course in life, then somehow there has got to be another way.

I am determined to find that way—and my only hope for survival seems to be with the Colony. It has a name that I'm not allowed to reveal, so I'll just call it the Colony. I like that. What an amazing place it must be.

I am beginning to collect my bare necessities—my clothing, my money, my paints. And I am ready to embark on a new life, a new adventure.

Probably.

In three days.

It's my only hope.

CHAPTER TEN: VIAGRA

I look back on the moment when I pulled out of my driveway three days later as the most significant turning point of my life. We don't often realize the lessons we're being taught as we're being taught them; and I will always be grateful to Dave for teaching me, then and later, what I most needed to learn.

My white Saturn was chock full of all my things. I had spent the whole day before getting packed and ready. It was the strangest feeling to choose what to take, not knowing if I'd ever return to my home. I had one final task to complete before I left: to write the note I would leave on my door. I wrote it in bright blue ink:

Dear Micky, Dave, or anyone else who might be concerned: I have decided to leave my life behind me. Please try not to worry, as I am going to a special place, but am not allowed to reveal where it is. I'm not sure when or if I'll return, as my life was not working for me here. Please don't try to find me. I am not permitted to contact you or reveal my whereabouts. Wish me well, as I do you, always. Love, Viagra.

I taped the note to my door and got into my car, not knowing if I'd ever see my house again. Or if I'd ever want to. I started the car after one false attempt, and the music came on to bid me goodbye: I couldn't believe it—it was Brahms again, his Fourth Symphony this time, just beginning as I pulled away. To this day, whenever I hear it, I always remember the morning I left my house, my neighborhood—and my sad, yet optimistic journey toward the Colony, seven hours away.

If you'd like to know the mood of my first hour of driving, please listen to this music. It captures my lilting joy, my hidden desperation, my longing for something... intangible? My need to die and be reborn into a

41

new life. The nobility of a journey toward the unknown.

I was afraid; I wasn't able to eat; I hadn't been able to sleep. I knew I was headed where I needed to go—but had no idea if I could survive in this new environment—or what the people would be like. I felt like a child on my first day of school—or my first day of summer camp, which was worse.

It was my first day of girls camp and I couldn't eat my peanut butter sandwich on the bus with all the butterflies in my stomach. I sat next to a counselor who kept saying, "Oh, we play a lot of tennis at camp!" And I wasn't especially fond of tennis. When the bus finally pulled into the camp, they couldn't find my bunk—I didn't exist! I wasn't on the list! I bravely held back my tears, while my friend Marla cried for me—and made sure they found my bunk.

I hoped this experience was going to be better than that camp.

I was on the highway going north. The hills and valleys seemed to match the mystery of the music. Overhead was a mixture of blue sky and white, fluffy clouds, ready to catch me like a safety net, should I fall from heaven. I started to feel a little happy with my vision of the clouds, the music that I loved, and my drive toward my destiny. How I loved music more than anything. More than life, that was for sure.

I remembered hearing that Brahms's First Piano Concerto was so poorly received, it took him ten years to begin work on his First Symphony. I could understand that. The world was cruel and wanted to prevent you from being yourself, from creating anything new or different. The world wanted to kill you, wanted to stop you dead in your tracks. And they nearly succeeded with me, I thought, as I passed by green farms with black and white cows, standing and eating grass. Good—they were standing, an optimistic sign. My mother always said if they were lying down, it meant rain.

My head was becoming clear. I felt like I was on an important journey. What a great alternative to suicide. But where was I going to sleep? Would they find my bunk? Would I have a friend to cry for me? Would I be able to paint again? Would my work equal the other artists' there?

I tried not to be overwhelmed with worries. I tried to use the drive as an experience in transformation. As long as music existed, somehow I could live; the great composers understood me, even if no one else did. If I could have music, I could survive anything. Wasn't Brahms always triumphant in the end?

Here was the dramatic part of the second movement, similar to the fate themes of Beethoven and Tchaikovsky. The great ones knew how to do it. They really knew how to reach you. You just had to listen, to travel with the music, let it lead you—and nothing could steer you wrong.

Then came my first turn of many. The music was a soundtrack that lifted the trip to something significant. Well, it *was* significant. Ah, the third movement was exuberant! Did I ever know sadness?

I had forgotten.

I started imagining the paintings I'd paint when I was at the Colony. Huge canvases—huge masterpieces—why not? If Brahms could do it, so could I. Why not be ambitious? I would paint enormous canvases with the boldest of colors. I would express my soul, my pain, my longing to explode with jubilation—like the music!

But what could I paint with my bold strokes of color?

And then it dawned on me: I would paint my father beating me. I would paint a man with a black, leather belt beating a naked girl of five. Such a chill I experienced as I knew this would be my theme.

The last movement started but I was already cured; my idea had been created. Now the work had to begin: the determination, the discipline, the painstaking, every-day stroking, gliding, of the paint on canvas. I knew I could do it. I felt completely confident. I'd never felt that way before: I had an original idea.

I will exorcize my childhood trauma, I thought. I will transform it into art, into music. I will make my pain a thing of beauty. And I will be redeemed for it. Amen.

The music had gotten quiet; I thought I might need to stop for a restroom. I forgot what was coming next—the quiet before the storm? The uncertainty after all that joy? I decided to stop after the symphony finished.

The driving on the road hypnotized me. I was in a trance of freedom, a trance of the spirit. I drove toward my deliverance. Ah, here it comes, I thought: the music swelled and foreshadowed something thrilling: a new romance? No, something bigger. Something greater. My paintings. My canvases. Large and strong. Audacious and brave.

I was not afraid. I was steady, I was sure. The past was dead. The future was clear. The present moved toward the future: to stay alive, to exalt in my work, my self, born on that day. That day after three days of knowing: this was my road, my fate, my freedom.

Ah, the artist in me, my epiphany! Here, now, in this music!

And then it ended—so abruptly.

It was time to pull over....

Six hours later I slowly approached a road at the bottom of a hill and turned right onto it. There were trees everywhere; it was like being in the middle of a deserted forest. The gravel of the unpaved road churned in my wheels, preparing me for the great ascent ahead. I climbed the road that swerved and swaggered upward, like a secret path to a treasure. I veered to the right and then to the left; the climb evened out and then got steep again. I drove higher and higher in my Saturn with my belongings and supplies. The road seemed like it would never end.

But finally I approached the top of the hill. There was a huge rock that stood directly in my path, forcing me to drive around it, either to the left or to the right. And on the rock these words were painted in white letters:

Whosoever dares to venture beyond this point may make a great mistake. But as with all mistakes in life, it may prove to be a valuable one. Do you pledge unto yourself a life of integrity? For those of you who dare to drive further, that is what you are about to undertake. Drive further if you dare—but only if you have courage. For it takes great courage to discover who you are. Welcome to the _____ Colony.

Without hesitation, I turned my steering wheel to the right and drove ahead.

CHAPTER ELEVEN: VIOLET

Was it my imagination? Did everything suddenly get brighter beyond that rock? Perhaps it was simply a clearing of the trees and the late afternoon sunlight shining through. At any rate, it seemed a lot brighter and I felt like a new woman.

I realized that I was no longer Viagra and decided to introduce myself with a new name. I immediately chose Violet, the name of my favorite doll as a little girl. She wasn't just a pretty doll, she was the smart one. And the word "violet" alluded to the highest spiritual color of the spectrum. I was now Violet—no more snickers every time I introduced myself.

There was a sign that said: *Congratulations. You are here. Please park in the lot ahead and come to the office on your left.*

It looked like a kind of camp. There were cabins of different sizes on both sides of the road; and some had murals painted on them. One had dancers in a circle, like a Matisse painting. I would discover later that each was a particular art shop, focusing on a different specialty: the Sculpture Shop, the Silver Shop, the Painting Shack, etc. It all looked very attractive and welcoming. Still, the butterflies in my stomach hadn't let up; and I hadn't eaten anything all day.

I drove to the parking lot next to a tennis court. Oh no, I didn't want to play tennis there! Well, no one was playing; so maybe no one else wanted to play tennis either. I locked up my car with all my belongings, even though there was probably no need to do so, and started walking toward the office.

On the path to the office, I passed a young man with curly red hair who gave me the sweetest smile, as if to say, "Hello, I'm so glad you're here today!" I smiled right back, wondering who he could be.

The office was next to a large porch. I walked up to the window and started to talk: "Hello, my name is Violet. Hans is expecting me, but he knows me as Viagra—I just changed my name."

And the woman, who had an English accent, said, "Oh we're used to that, darling. A lot of people change their names on their journey to get here."

At that moment, a loud gong went off, ringing over and over, practically in my ear. I turned around and saw someone striking what looked like a large train wheel with a mallet. It was hanging from a rectangular post, just next to the porch.

"That's the trademark of our Colony," said the woman. "They're sounding the gong. It's time for tea."

Suddenly everyone starting lining up on the porch to receive their tea and shortbread, it looked like. There was Hans, much older than the rest of them. With all the excitement, I almost forgot to explain my new identity.

"Hans!" I cried, rushing over to him. "Before you introduce me to anyone, I've changed my name."

"I've been expecting that, my dear," he said, with a fairly thick German accent. "Most people change their names when they come here. What is your new name?"

"It's Violet. It came to me just after I drove by the big rock."

"Everyone, quiet please," he announced. "This is Violet, just arrived from a long journey, seven hours away. She is here to stay with us for a while. Let us welcome her."

Everyone smiled and started applauding; they were a young, attractive bunch—much younger than I expected. A handsome, dark-haired man named Max came right over and offered me some tea.

"Hello, Violet. I'm Max. Would you like some tea?"

"Oh, thank you, Max, I think I would."

"And how about a shortbread cookie? I'm sure you haven't eaten anything all day. None of us did on our trips here. We were all so frightened! But as you can see, we're a harmless bunch—a little crazy, but harmless."

An older woman approached me. "My darling Violet, welcome to this magic place. We are so glad to have you with us. My name is Aurelia—truly—though it is not my real name. I changed it when I arrived, too. And coincidence or no, I happen to be playing the lead role tonight in *The Madwoman of Chaillot*, the Countess Aurelia! Do you know how lucky you are to catch our first performance? Wait till you see our theatre! We will give you the seat of honor."

"I have taken a peek at rehearsals, Violet," said Hans, "and I will tell you, it promises to be a very special evening. So how was your drive, my dear? You found us okay?"

"Oh yes," I said breathlessly, trying to sip my tea. "It was a beautiful drive and the music on the radio was like a film soundtrack—very inspiring."

"You'll have to hear our small orchestra. They're giving a concert later in the week—an all Schumann program, I believe?"

"Schubert, darling, Schubert," said Aurelia.

"Ah, of course…I always get them confused. I should know better, with my background! Ah, Erda, here is Violet…she's changed her name, of course."

Erda approached me with tears in her eyes and started putting daisies in my hair.

"Welcome, dear Violet," she said, also with an accent. "I wish I had violets to honor you, but these will have to do. We hope you feel at home with us."

"Oh, Erda, I'm starting to. It seems like a wonderful place."

"Filled with all of us wonderful people!" laughed Max.

"You ought to see Max's sculptures—and you will soon, I'm sure," said Hans. "I am personally in awe of him. He has already sold two."

"Really? Where?" I asked.

"Once a week we have a show in the town," replied Hans. "That's how we're able to support ourselves. We retain our anonymity, of course, yet people come from far and wide to buy our art. They don't know it's from us, though; the dealer makes sure of that. But his reputation draws people from all over the world. And the atmosphere here encourages

47

only the best work, which is what we expect from you—nothing less."

"Well," I said, "I'm up for the challenge. I just got inspired, driving here. And I'm looking forward to it a lot."

"Let's not excite Violet too much on her first day," said Erda. "She must be exhausted. Let me show you where you'll be staying. Would you like that, my dear? We can bring your car around while you unload. Dinner will be at seven, just after the gong, and then the performance is at eight-thirty—not to be missed!"

"Hear, hear!" a few people exclaimed.

"We're all in it," a young blond woman grinned.

"All right, everybody, let's let Violet unpack and relax," smiled Hans. "We'll have plenty of time to impress her later."

"Thank you all," I said, trying not to choke up too soon, "Thank you for making me feel so welcome."

"Oh, you're welcome!" said Max.

"Come along, darling," said Erda, taking my hand.

"Bye, everyone, see you later, I guess."

"You'll see me on the great stage!" winked Aurelia. "Lovely to meet you, dear."

And Erda led me away from the porch, away from the tea, away from perhaps the best bunch of people I had ever met.

Not only did they find my bunk—for it really was like a summer camp for adults—but there were freshly-cut flowers awaiting me on my dresser and a modest supply of sheets and towels. I was to be sharing my bunk with three women in the Women's Annex, it was called. Erda helped me unload my car and then she left me to unpack, relax, and shower before dinner. The showers and restrooms were down the hall.

For a first day somewhere new and foreign, I felt relatively at home. I unpacked quickly, knowing just where I wanted all my things; and I left the painting materials in the car for another day. I tried to lie down for a little while but since I was so excited—and still quite nervous—I wasn't able to sleep at all.

I decided to shower—it took some time for the hot water to come on—and got myself feeling pretty refreshed. Before I knew it, I heard the gong for dinner; so I bravely left my new home (I hadn't yet met my bunkmates; I wondered where they were) and ventured off in the direction of the dining room, next to the porch.

It felt as if I were in a dream world; and I tried to enjoy the new experience instead of being overwhelmed by it. I kept reminding myself that this was an alternative to suicide—and what a pleasant alternative it was.

There were about thirty people in the dining room when I arrived. Max waved and motioned me over; he was saving me a seat. I must say, I did feel a little jittery; I didn't know how I was going to eat—or how good the food could possibly be. But Max immediately cracked a joke:

"Now Violet, you've got to eat everything on your plate because we have a gourmet chef here who will be very insulted if you don't like his cooking!" And then he whispered in my ear, "It's really not that bad... just take a deep breath and say, 'I'm hungry. This is delicious. I've got a voracious appetite.' And you should have no problem at all."

And it really seemed to work; I was able to eat and it wasn't half bad. Pork chops and spinach. Not bad at all. And apple pie with vanilla ice cream for dessert. Really not bad at all!

After dessert, Hans climbed up on the platform at the side of the dining room and looked like he was about to make a speech:

"Tonight we would like to thank Grego for his cataclysmic dinner..."

Everyone started laughing.

"...oh, is that the wrong choice of word? Better change it to... *orgasmic* dinner!"

Everyone laughed again.

"...and Ventura for supplying the Haydn String Quartet recordings. (I hadn't even noticed the music with all the excitement, to tell the truth.) And again we would like to welcome Violet and congratulate her for making it through her first dinner with us. The first of many, we hope.

"I know that all of you are getting excited about tonight's performance of *The Madwoman of Chaillot*, which will be starting in approximately one half hour. I suggest that those of you who want coffee or tea to get it now, as the performance is not a short one; and we will not permit snoring during the action. That simply will not do!"

They all laughed and Max whispered to me, "That's one of Hans's expressions. He knows that we joke about it, so now he says it in a self-mocking way."

"I see," I replied with an amused look on my face.

"And so, my friends," he continued, "we will see you at the theatre after the gong. Please be on time, as latecomers will not be admitted, even though it is out-of-doors, as you know, and would be easy to sneak in. But that certainly would not do. See you soon."

Everyone started taking their trays and dishes over to a conveyor belt and then we began to stroll *en masse* toward the theatre. And what a splendid sight it was when I first laid my eyes upon it. Reminiscent of an open-air Greek theatre in miniature, there were multi-colored lights hitting the proscenium from all angles; and several tiers of seats led down to the stage in a semi-circle. I descended the steps with a sense of wonder.

Erda was there, saving my "seat of honor," and she motioned for me to come over.

"Did you enjoy your dinner, my dear?"

"Oh, Erda, I was actually able to eat. Thank you for being so generous. It was good."

"We try our best with the food, Violet. But it's the art—and the theatre—that we're truly proud of here. Tomorrow you'll get to see everyone's work. But enjoy this tonight. This is one of the special pleasures of the _____ Colony; so it's lucky that you arrived in time for the premiere."

I heard the gong, which was becoming quite a charming sound already, and everyone rushed in to take their seats.

Hans came on the stage to make an announcement:

"In keeping with our theme of integrity at the _____ Colony, we would like to offer you tonight *The Madwoman of Chaillot* by Jean Giraudoux. It is a play about humanity, and as you shall see, it shows a

50

beautiful, if idealistic way to live in this 'cold, cruel world,' much as we do here in our little utopian society. Pay attention to what the madwomen tell you, for perhaps they are not so mad at all. We hope you enjoy."

After the applause, I was transported into a magical and whimsical world. I was transfixed from the first moment by the colorful lighting and enchanting music; but as the play unfolded, a story of four madwomen who get rid of all the evil people in the world, I knew by the end of the performance that I had chosen the right place to be.

We all stood and bravoed and cried. I couldn't believe how professional it was. And when Aurelia came out for her bow, wearing her flamboyant hat and feather boa, everyone cheered. I simply had not expected a first day like this!

I headed back to my bunk feeling a little sad that all the excitement was over; and I finally met my bunkmates, who seemed to respect my need for quiet and getting a good first night's sleep. They were very sweet but didn't say much; they sat in bed reading before the final gong, which meant lights out; and I lay on my cot, which was small yet solid, and started to cry a little.

I cried for all the madwomen and madmen of the world, who wanted it to be a better place; I cried for Micky, I cried for Dave. And I cried for Viagra, who was no more, who would live only as a little girl in the paintings I would create, as magical and colorful as an outdoor theatre, a theatre of the imagination, where the world could be a beautiful, good, and happy place.

I fell into a deep sleep and dreamed of black and white cows flying over the moon, smiling and singing like madwomen...until a gong somewhere in the distance told me that the moon had disappeared and morning had arrived.

CHAPTER TWELVE: DAVE

I'm still trying to get over what Micky told me. How could it be true? That Viagra hears voices? That she's...schizophrenic? She might have seemed a little sad to me, but I can't imagine her being crazy or anything—and is this the girl I thought I was falling in love with?

I'm all confused. I never had anything like this happen to me before. I've been trying to decide what to do about it. I haven't been able to call her—I don't know how to handle it. Normally, I would've called her or seen her by now—but the whole thing has turned me upside down and made me wonder what kind of woman I can love. What *is* love anyway? Could I be crazy myself?

I can't stand this anymore. Let me pull over and call Micky. See if he can answer some of my questions....

"Hi. This is Micky. Please don't hang up. I might be screening this call to avoid negative people. There are too many around. So please state your name and if I'm here, perhaps I will pick up. Thanks for understanding."

"Micky? Hey, it's Dave...."

"Dave! How are you, man? I was just thinking about you!"

"Listen. I've been a little messed up since I saw you."

"Oh. Hope the incident in the car didn't turn you off or anything."

"No, nothing about that. It's Viagra. I'm trying to understand—and I don't know what to do about it. I've never met someone who was... schizophrenic before."

"I know what you mean. Well, what do you want to know?"

"Well, for starters, what about these voices she hears? What kind of voices are they?"

"Uh...they're children's voices."

"Children's voices?"

"That's right. See, our parents died when we were very young—and she keeps hearing the little brother and sister crying out for their lost parents."

"But I thought she had a different father than you."

"Yeah, she did; but we grew up in the same house. And after our parents died, we used to wait by the front door, crying and begging for them to come back. But they never came back. So I think it's *our* voices she hears—crying out for our parents."

"Whoa...this is really heavy. It's so sad. I would never guess this about Viagra. How did your parents die?"

"Um...Dave...I don't like to talk about it that much, if that's OK. Do you understand?"

"Sure. Well, does Viagra tell people? Does she take medicine for this? Does she see a doctor?"

"I think she likes to keep it pretty secret. But I thought it was important that you know. Yeah, she's on medication—it makes her pretty normal."

"Jeez—I still can't believe this. I've been very upset about it. Do you think I should talk to her?"

"If I were you, I wouldn't mention it. It's something the two of us never discuss and I think it would embarrass her."

"Well, damn. This is a fucking lousy position I'm in. I can't tell her about it and it makes me feel uncomfortable. I feel uncomfortable with myself! I'm gonna have to talk to someone."

"What are you doing tonight? Do you want to swing by? Are you in the area?"

"I'm about an hour away. I could do that."

"Good. It would be good to see you again. And we can talk if you like."

"OK. How about ten-thirty? Do you have any coffee?"

"Yeah, the best."

"Good. I'll need some. What's your address, anyway?"

"Number 8, View Drive, just off 99. Exit 3. You know it?"

"Yeah. See you around ten-thirty then."

"Great, Dave, see you later."

Good. So I'll get to work this out a little in my mind. Micky's a good person to talk to. Very smart. Knows things. I've got to figure this out tonight. Maybe, if I feel together enough, I'll swing by Viagra's house after that. I sure would like to see her. I just don't know what to say to her.

Maybe I'll know later....

CHAPTER THIRTEEN: MICKY

I couldn't believe it. Dave finally called. And he was coming to see me, not Viagra. Did I have any qualms about telling him what I did? That was hard to say. I did what I had to do. What I thought was necessary. What I thought was true at the time.

We do what we do to get by in life. Who's to say whether it's right or wrong? We do what we do to survive. All of us. We tell the truth or we tell lies as it suits us. No one is immune to this sad philosophy. Life is too hard. We do what we need to do when we need to do it.

And I say, Hail to the man who makes his world his own. Hail to the woman who knows how to get what she needs. There is no judgment involved; life is too short—the list of worries is too long. We live to get by and we get by with what we can.

If I had it to do over, would I have told Dave what I did?

How can I say that? We get one chance, at least this time around. We take what we get and give back what we take. Nothing is fair; nothing makes sense. Except for one thing: we do what we need to do. There is no good or evil in this world. Only people trying to get what they know they must have.

I thought maybe I'd have time for a quick meditation before Dave came over. Only problem was, how could I possibly sit still? Sometimes the sitting still posed quite a problem. I really had to be in a somewhat relaxed state.

So I abandoned the idea of meditation and decided to shower instead. I decided not to shave; I wanted to look as masculine as possible. I wanted to be the strong, masculine, intelligent one, someone Dave could look up to for advice, someone he'd need to return to again and again.

Don't judge me, I ask you, as I tell you the truth of my soul. Who do you think you are? Jesus, Buddha, Mohammed all rolled into one? Are you developing opinions about me already? Without even hearing half of my story yet? Please chill out. You know nothing about me.

Remember, I can read your mind if and when I so desire, so watch out that you don't think bad thoughts about me. I'll detect them and boomerang them back on you! So read my story, but try not to judge me, all right? Because those who judge, especially the psychological types, are the ones who need the most judgment of all. Sorry if I sound over-existential.

Dave rang my bell—and boy, was I thrilled. It was the most exciting thing to happen in two and a half weeks. He came up, we shook hands, I poured him my special brew of coffee, and he started his interrogation:

"So what does it really mean to be schizophrenic?" he asked.

"It's a form of psychosis," I said. "Most of us these days are neurotic to some degree, but we manage to cope with reality. Someone who's psychotic blurs the borderline between fantasy and reality."

"But who's to say what is the real reality, the real fantasy?"

"Good question, Dave. I don't know the answer to that. The psychologists and psychiatrists, I guess. They think they know."

"Have you ever been to one?"

"Of course. Hasn't everyone?"

"Not me."

"Well, you're very together. One of the more together guys I've known."

"Well, I haven't been feeling very together lately. What you told me has really fucked me up. Forced me to question who I am, you know?"

"You must be a very sensitive man then."

"How so?"

"Well, most guys would have just split the scene after what I told you. But you used it for a process of self-questioning, even though it had nothing really to do with you. That's very impressive and says a lot for your sensitivity as a man."

"You really think so?"

"I know so."

"So what can I do to be fair and sensitive to Viagra?"

"Only you can answer that, Dave. You've got to proceed with the knowledge you have. How do you feel about her? Did it change after what I told you?"

"These are the questions I've been trying to figure out."

"They're good questions. Keep asking them."

"What gets me is this one: is it OK to love someone who may be crazy—and does that make *you* crazy? I know that doesn't make total sense, but it's how I feel, or at least how I've been feeling."

"We're all a little crazy to some degree. That's what makes life interesting."

"Yeah, but I mean really crazy."

"Maybe it doesn't matter at all, if you love someone. Or think you do. But to *think* you do is the same as *if* you do."

"Huh?"

"Think about it."

"Oh...yeah."

"So, what's the verdict?"

I sat next to him on the couch and put my hand on his thigh.

"Hey, man," he said. "I've got nothing against that—but not tonight. I've got to figure this out. I've got to see Viagra."

"Are you sure this is the best time? It's a little late for her, you know."

"No, I've got to do it. It's been too long. Thanks for the coffee. I'm sure I'll be seeing you again soon. I'll let you know what happens."

"OK, Dave. You're an adult. You're a helluva man. You've made a decision. I can respect that."

"Thanks. So listen, I'll call you in a while. Let you know what's up."

"You do that, sir. I'll look forward to it."

"Take care, man."

He shook my hand and was off.

Damn.

Remember what I said. Don't judge me. Look at yourself in the mirror and judge yourself. But don't judge me. You might regret it someday.

I wondered if I should call Viagra and let her know that Prince Charming was on his way. No, I decided, I'd let her be surprised. One of us, at least, ought to have a surprising night. But the joke was on me and Dave: *we* were the ones who would be truly surprised.

And I'll never forget the impact of that surprise when I discovered Dave at my door about an hour and a half later—drunk, in tears, and begging me to let him back in.

CHAPTER FOURTEEN: VIOLET

The smell of the oil paint in the Painting Shack took me back to a time I had almost forgotten. I was a young girl of eleven, and Micky, who was thirteen, had set me up in a small studio, a little shack that was close to our house. It was in the middle of a deserted field full of daisies. The smell as I entered the Painting Shack for the first time took me right back there unexpectedly.

T.S. Elliot had a term for it: *objective correlative*. When something through the senses—a smell, a taste, a piece of music—takes you back to another time. Music has always had that effect on me.

So when I smelled that special smell, I immediately felt at home—much more at home than I felt in the Sculpture Shop, for instance; though it was pretty amazing seeing Max's sculptures. They were giant women carved in white plaster, all of them goddesses towering over us. He had to stand on a ladder most of the time, especially when he worked on their heads. I was really impressed. And I felt attracted to Max as well. I hadn't been sure if he was gay or not; but when I saw his female nudes, I hoped that he might be straight. That was all I needed, right? To have an affair with Max at the Colony? Well, I was sure that stranger things had happened there.

A man named Geramund helped me set up my easel and we began to stretch a large canvas. Max's sculpture had inspired me; but I already had the idea to make my paintings very large, as I told you. Geramund started joking with me—or so I thought: "I hope your subject matter is going to equal the size of your paintings, Violet. Remember, the theme matters. Picasso didn't paint *Guernica* in a day!"

He had sandy, blond hair with a reddish moustache, one end of which curled up and the other which curled down.

"Oh, I don't plan on painting my masterpiece in a day, Geramund..."

"Please, call me Geram for short, Vi."

"I'll call you Geram if you like, but please call me Violet. It's too new to start playing around with it. I hardly know myself as Violet yet."

"Well, excuse me," he said with a bit of an attitude.

I didn't know if I liked Geramund—he was the first person at the Colony I wasn't crazy about. And of course, I'd be working side by side with him. Ah, potential conflict! I'd better be careful, I thought, try to have a sense of humor.

"So, Geram," I said casually, "do you think I'll be able to have some privacy? It's going to be a very personal work and I won't be ready to show it for a while."

"Oh, I can take a hint, Violet. I can take a hint. Now that you're all set up and ready to go, I'll just leave and go to my side of the shack. I won't bother you again...until you need something, like borrowing my very rare, imported Mandarin Orange—have you ever heard of it? Very rare. Makes for a sensational sunset, if you're planning to have sunsets."

"Probably not, but if I do, I'll holler."

"OK, toodle-loo."

Oh gosh, I had to work with this person? Maybe this wasn't such a utopia after all.

But at that moment Max came in, as if to rescue me.

"Violet, I'm glad to see we'll have to look up to your painting! I've always believed in Big Art. Art should make the viewer a bigger person, don't you think?"

"Yes," I realized, "I've always felt that way."

"And wouldn't you know, according to Feng Shui, you've chosen the place of fame in the Painting Shack? Whoever paints their painting right in your spot is destined for fame. Nothing you do can interfere. Just paint—you'll see."

"Oh, please," whined Geramund from the other side of the shack. "Let's not get Feng Shuied again! Did you notice the Sculpture Shop— mirrors everywhere? It's a conspiracy!"

"Just a little something I've gotten into recently," explained Max. "I enjoy it, and it's stylish, too. But really, Violet, you've chosen the place for fame, so your destiny is upon you, here in the Painting Shack."

"I don't know what to say, Max. I don't know anything about Feng Shui, but maybe you can teach me."

"He's got goldfish in the Men's Annex!" shouted Geramund.

"Yeah, we enjoy them, Geramund! They're aesthetically pleasing. You oughta come over some evening and help with the feeding. You just might enjoy yourself for a change."

"I've got better things to do than play with goldfish. I'm reading Rimbaud."

"My word, Violet. How can we compete with Rimbaud?"

"Am I going to be able to paint with him around?" I whispered.

"Just politely set your boundary and he'll respect that. He's really harmless, just has a little chip on his shoulder and hasn't sold anything yet. Sometimes some of us can get a little competitive here; but you just do your work—do it from your heart—and no one will interfere with that."

"Thanks, Max, that sounds reasonable, just what I plan to do."

"Good. Well, I just wanted to check in on you. I'm back to molding my ears, my least favorite part of the anatomy, I think. But once I get them out of the way, I can really go wild with what I call my Medusa hair! Can't wait for that—see you later?"

"At lunch?"

"It's a date."

I blushed, I think. He really was handsome—and straight. Definitely straight!

"Thanks for coming by, Max. I'll see you later. After I get inspired."

"You seem like you're in a constant state of inspiration. At least, you're very inspiring—to me, that is. Oh, I should just go before putting my foot in it. Bye, Violet."

"Bye, Max," I smiled. We definitely had a chemistry thing going.

Meanwhile, Geramund was making funny noises with his tongue. I was going to have to learn to deal with him.

I mustered all my concentration and got ready.

I was Viagra again. I was five years old. I was in the bathroom taking a bath. And my father burst through the door and started yelling at me. Let me start with the water—that's it—the water in the tub, that's where I'll begin.

I was splashing in the water, playing with my duck. My duck named Boo-Boo. He'll be in the painting too. It'll be the only yellow, the only happy color. Suddenly my daddy, my England daddy, burst through the door and shouted, "What are you doing in there, Viagra? You're supposed to be with Mummy. Mummy says she can't find you."

"But Micky told her! Micky told her I'm in the bathtub!" I started to cry.

"Don't lie to me, you spoiled girl. Don't lie to the only real father you've got. Don't you ever lie to me." He came over real close and was ready to hit me.

"But I'm not lying, Daddy! I'm not lying!" I was really crying now.

And then he whacked me real hard across the side of my face.

The waters of my bath became violent, more like an ocean storm than a calm bathtub. That's how I would paint it: like an ocean storm.

I spent the rest of the morning with the turbulent blues and greens of the water, which would give my painting its emotional depth. The waters of the deep sorrow that was my childhood, the waters of my pain and humiliation—it would all be in this painting; and I, Violet, would be released from my past.

For I was in the place of fame. And I knew that this beginning would lead me to it.

CHAPTER FIFTEEN: DAVE

You might like to know a little more about me, a little more about my past. But the trouble is, I don't remember any of it. I don't remember anything before about ten years ago. As far as I can tell, I've been driving my truck my whole life. I just don't remember doing anything else.

Could I have amnesia or something? I don't know. I don't know where I come from. Sorry to disappoint you, but that's the truth of my life. I don't even remember my childhood, if I ever had one. Or who my parents were. For all I know, I'm from another planet.

I live in the present and that makes me feel free.

At least I thought I was free until I got mixed up with Viagra and Micky and this whole situation.

It was about fifteen minutes from Micky's to Viagra's. I was really looking forward to seeing her. I missed her. I felt bad about staying away for so long, even with what I found out. I kind of wished I just went to her, talked about it. Honesty is always best, you know? But I didn't do that—so I was feeling bad.

Still, I was excited about seeing her and hoped I wouldn't wake her up or something. When I got to her house, none of the lights were on, so I parked my truck in the street and went up the path to her door. But when I got to the door, there was this note on it. I couldn't read it in the dark, so I pulled it off and went back to my truck. I read the note inside. And I couldn't believe it—Viagra was gone—and it was probably my fault.

I felt real bad, worse than I ever felt before. I mean *real* bad. I didn't know what to do, so I drove to the country and western place where we met a while back and had a drink, a J.D. on the rocks. I took out my smokes, my Marlboros, and tried to figure out what was going on. There were a few pretty girls there who were looking at me. But I didn't want to talk to them. I just felt real bad.

But one of them came up to me and said, "Hi there, I'm Janet. How are you doin' tonight, stranger?"

"Hi Janet," I said, "I'm not too good. Sorry, don't feel much like talking."

"What's the matter, handsome? Some lady got you down?"

"Yeah, that's it. How could you tell?"

"Written all over your face. Well, why don't I help you to forget about her?"

"You know, Janet, I'm not usually like this—but I got myself into this situation and I really don't know what to do about it."

"Well sometimes it's best to just let these things ride, you know? Figure them out another time?" She started putting her hand through my hair.

"Hey listen, baby, I told you, this is not the best time for me."

"You've really got it bad for her, I can tell. What's your name, sad man?"

"Dave."

"Hi, Dave. What happened? Did she leave you for another man?"

"No, nothing like that. I thought I loved her but found out she was crazy."

"Crazy?"

"Yeah, really crazy, hearing voices and everything. I didn't know what to do, so I didn't do anything, and now I just found out that she left. Left her house, don't know where she's going. All because of me probably. I feel really bad."

"You're so sweet, Dave. You're like a little kid. Where did you grow up?"

"I don't remember. You want a drink?"

"Sure...what do you mean, you don't remember?"

"Just what I said, I don't remember. I have no idea where I grew up."

"Sounds like you're the crazy one."

"You know, Janet, I don't need to hear this right now. I've got to think about this, figure this out, OK?"

"OK, Dave, you crazy canary. I'll leave you alone. If you want a good time, I'll be playing pool." And she finally left.

I ordered another J.D. and lit another smoke. What was I going to do? I felt like I could lose it right then and there. A song came on the jukebox—or did I imagine it? Did I make it up?

Why do I feel crazy without you?

Why do I feel so blue?

Why am I so crazy?

Alone, missing you?

Fuck. I felt like I could just start to cry. I had to get out of there.

I gulped down the rest of my drink, put out my butt and went outside to the parking lot. Three pretty girls were laughing and waving at me. But I was crying. I didn't know what to do. I felt like a total asshole. You have to understand, I wasn't used to feeling this way.

I got in my truck and read the note again. Then I really started bawling. What was I going to do? I could think of only one thing. I would head on back to Micky's. I was in no shape to drive very far anyway. So I started up and drove very carefully down the highway towards Micky's house. I was sure he wouldn't mind if I spent the night.

I parked in the driveway next to his Camaro (my rig jutted out into the street a little) and went up to the door. I started knocking. "Micky!" I yelled. "Let me back in, OK? Micky...are you there? Micky, it's me— Dave—can you let me back in?"

"Dave, is that you?" He peered through the glass in the door.

"Yeah, it's me. Let me in. OK?"

He opened the door and said, "What's the matter, man? You look a little messed up."

"Yeah. I found this note at Viagra's." I was still crying. I felt like a jerk.

Micky read the note but didn't say anything. He just looked very glad to see me. "Well, come in. Let me get you a drink. I can tell you want one."

"Got any whiskey?"

"Of course. You like Jack Daniels?"

"How did you know?"

"I can read your mind. Come on in...have a seat. I'll just be a sec. Put on some music if you like."

"Thanks." I turned on the radio and the classical station was on. They were playing something very relaxing. It was good to be back there. I felt safe there. I felt like I could talk to Micky.

"Here you are, partner. J.D. Ice OK?"

"Sure. Real good...aaah. Listen, you mind if I sleep over? I've had a few and shouldn't drive."

"No problem, sir. I was just getting ready for bed.... You want to join me?"

"I think I'd like that."

"Well, I'd like it too," he said, putting his hand on my shoulder.

"My mind is just swimming with all of this," I said. "I'm glad you're here. It's good to be here."

And then something happened that I didn't expect. But I didn't mind it or anything. Micky, with his hand still on my shoulder, leaned over to me and started kissing me on my mouth. It was the first time a guy had ever done that to me. But feeling the way I was feeling, with the J.D. and everything, I have to say, it felt good. It felt strong. It felt like I was going to be OK.

We kissed for a little while—man to man kissing—strange, but nice, you know? Nice, like a new experience, like having a new kind of friend. And then he put his hand out and took mine, real strong, like guys, you know, and led me with his goofy-looking smile in the direction of his bedroom.

I was looking forward to being safe there with Micky, at least for a while...until I could make sense out of everything. I was with my new friend and everything was going to be all right.

CHAPTER SIXTEEN: VIOLET

My first day of work at the Colony was much more productive than I ever would have imagined. There was something about the atmosphere that seemed to inspire good work. Or maybe it was my place of fame that did it. But whatever the reason, by the end of the afternoon, after a nice lunch with Max, whom I was growing fonder of by the minute, I was off to an unusually good start.

There was nothing like the feeling of working unencumbered, without the restrictions of a conventional work routine; and having the opportunity to concentrate, despite Geramund's occasional annoyances, I was able to achieve something with the water that I didn't even know was in me. I was very pleased by the end of the day.

I washed my hands in the sink, having made sure that my painting was turned around and covered so that no one could take a peek prematurely. "Bye-bye, Geramund, see you later," I waved, as I left the Painting Shack late in the afternoon.

"See you tomorrow, Violet—or perhaps at dinner, if you're lucky," he answered as I was halfway out the door.

I strolled back to the Women's Annex, marveling over the place they called the _____ Colony, realizing how fortunate I was to be a part of it. It looked like all the cabins were built in the middle of a secret forest that only the truly privileged were lucky enough to discover. It seemed to be an enchanted place of sorts. I passed by the theatre where a few people were cleaning the stage, getting ready for the second performance of *Madwoman*, as they called it. I didn't think I wanted to see it again; and Max had suggested that the two of us go for a walk after dinner—he wanted to show me this beautiful field. I fantasized what might take place in this beautiful field.

Just then I passed by the young man with the curly red hair who had made me feel so welcome in my first moments there. "Hello," I said, "I'm Violet. What's your name?"

"I'm Arnie," he said with a twinkle in his eye. "Don't you recognize me?"

"Yes, from yesterday, when I first parked my car. Your smile made me feel so welcome."

"That's right—but guess again—you saw me after that, quite a bit, actually."

"I did?"

"Without a doubt."

"That's funny; I don't remember seeing you after that."

"Should I give you a hint?"

"All right."

He suddenly became very theatrical, his speech more distinct: "Countess, the world has changed. The people are not the same. The people are different. There's been an invasion. From another planet. An infiltration. The world is not beautiful any more. It's not happy. There was a time when you could walk around Paris and all the people you met were just like yourself. A little cleaner, maybe, or dirtier, perhaps, or angry, or smiling—but you knew them. They were you."

He took my hand; and then he gestured in the air:

"Countess, twenty years ago, one day, on the street, I saw a face in the crowd. A face, you might say, without a face. The eyes—empty. The expression—not human. Not a human face.... Do you know who I am now?"

"The Ragpicker?"

"That's right," he grinned.

"My God! You look so different!"

"I know! I love not being recognized. I was wearing lots of makeup and a black wig."

"You were terrific, Arnie. I can't believe that was you."

"Are you coming to see us again tonight?"

"I'm not sure, I don't think so. I was so blown away last night, I

68

think I need a little change of pace. I'm going for a walk to some field."

"Oh, the Elysian Field? That's what we call it."

"I didn't know it had a name, but it's over there somewhere," I said, pointing beyond the Women's Annex.

"Yeah, that's the one. That's where people go to do naughty things. You're safer at our theatre!"

"Oh, I had no idea. Well, I'll have to warn my friend about it then."

"Who's your friend?"

"Max."

"Oh, Max. Swell guy. Very talented. A real ladies' man."

"Is that bad?"

"No, not at all, he's a good man. Maybe you'll have better luck with him than I did. In fact, I'm sure you will if he's invited you to the Elysian Field!"

"Thanks for alerting me to this, Arnie. There's a lot to know around here."

"Anytime you want the dish, ask me; I know just about everything. Any questions?"

"Well, I'm not worried about Max, but what about this Geramund character? I have to work with him in the Painting Shack, and I'm just not sure about him."

"Oh, Geramund. He's a little, how shall I say, paranoid? I'd be a touch careful around him if I were you. He's a distant cousin of Erda's. That's how he got to be here. No one knows how talented he really is; and most of us were chosen for our talents in different areas. I'd be just a touch cautious about trusting him, that's all."

"Thanks for telling me. I've already felt uneasy around him. I can tell he's going to be a challenge to work with."

"Yeah, the trouble is, Hans and Erda love him; in their eyes he can do no wrong. So I'd try not to get on his bad side. He got someone kicked out of here once."

"Really? What happened?"

"There was a very talented painter here and my guess is that Geramund was jealous. I don't know the whole story, but it seems

69

like he might have made something up about this guy and gotten him arrested. Something about smoking weed behind the theatre? I'm not sure. Anyway, everyone does that, so it's no big deal. But the story goes that Geramund had something to do with it. And the poor guy had to go back to New York City."

"There's certainly a fair amount of intrigue here; I never would have guessed."

"Oh, like everywhere else in the world, we've got our problems and fuck-ups. Nothing's as perfect as it seems here; there's no such thing as a true utopia, much as Hans would like to believe that there is. Listen, it's late—and I've got to get to the theatre. We've got a few notes from last night."

"Nice talking with you, Arnie. Let's do it again soon."

"Definitely. Glad I ran into you. Careful in the Elysian Field, now."

"Thanks for warning me."

"Bye."

What a sweetheart. I was glad he liked guys. It seemed like my life was getting complicated enough.

I headed back to the Women's Annex with just enough time to relax before dinner...and my rendezvous with the handsome, adventurous Max.

It was uncanny to me how it was possible to be depressed one day, suicidal the next, and suddenly find oneself in a dream of a world that seemed to promise happiness. They should eliminate antidepressants and mental hospitals, I thought, and simply transport people to the environments in which they belonged.

Max took my hand as we strolled toward the Elysian Field. The sun was beginning to go down behind the trees, casting shadows of a purple hue onto our faces, giving our walk a slightly dreamlike quality, as if we were two characters in a romance novel, not really ourselves; but instead the hero and heroine of our own imaginations.

"What brought you here, Violet?" he asked.

"That's a good question. The futility of life, I suppose. I was unhappy.

I was depressed. Nothing seemed to work in my life. I had a difficult childhood, but I always managed to remain sane somehow, even with my bouts of depression. My brother's pretty crazy, though. We love each other and we're very close, so it was hard not to tell him where I was going. I just left a note on the door. What about you?"

"I was unhappy too. I was fed up with the commercial art world. I was fed up with the type of women I kept meeting out there. It's very hard in this day and age to meet someone who's right, who understands. Do you know what I mean? People are so superficial."

"I know exactly what you mean."

"Have you had many boyfriends?"

"A few. Nothing that really lasted. I thought I met someone recently, but I guess we didn't have enough in common. It seemed like we had something special, but, if I can say this, when I meet someone like you, I realize that I need to meet a man with more of a purpose in life. Someone with a higher aspiration, a higher artistic goal. Your sculptures have really inspired me."

"I'll take that as quite a compliment, coming from you. Here we are: this is the Elysian Field. Isn't it beautiful?"

I couldn't seem to answer the question; I felt as if I were in a movie, as if I were transported beyond time. The sunset was painting the sky with bold strokes of reds and oranges and violets; and the wind blew the tall grass practically into our faces as we approached the open field with a feeling of freedom and vigor.

"I'm speechless," I said, finally. "What a place this is. Thank you for showing it to me."

"You're a special woman, Violet. You deserve to see the most beautiful places in the world. I've always thought that this is one of them."

His eyes had the perfect combination of tenderness and strength. They fused with mine for a few moments and then he pulled me close to him and started kissing me. He tasted like pine trees—that's the only way I can describe it—fresh, natural, masculine. Kissing him was like a salvation, a reward for my suffering.

We kissed for a long time, his hands massaging my back and making me feel good all over: my hair, my face, my breasts. What a lover he was! We reclined in the grass and kept kissing on the ground, rolling over, smiling at each other, as it gradually got dark and the first stars began to appear.

This is what life is about, I thought, to feel good with a man in the Elysian Field. I could die here—and die happily.

"Violet?" he asked.

"Yes?"

"Did you hear something?"

"No, I don't think so, just your breathing...just the wind."

"I heard something over there. Something rustling."

"I didn't hear anything."

"Just a minute." He stood up and I could see his erection through his trousers, which made me desire him even more. He disappeared behind the tall grass behind me. And then I did hear something. I suddenly got a little scared. There was a definite sound somewhere in front of me. But I couldn't see who it was through the grass. It was pretty dark now and I suddenly felt a real pang of fear. A human figure approached me and I gasped.

"Hello, Violet," the figure said. It was Geramund.

"Geramund, what are you doing here?" I asked, trying to mask my fear.

"Just taking a stroll on a beautiful night, Violet."

And at that moment, thank God, Max reappeared. "Geramund," he said. "You scared us, creeping up on us like that. You shouldn't do that. Please...go away. I'm spending some time with Violet."

"I can see that, Max. I can see that. Sorry to intrude. I'll be on my way. Final gong is in twenty minutes...better not miss it...."

"Goodbye, Geramund," said Max, very firmly.

"Goodbye, Violet," he said, disappearing once again.

"He really gives me the creeps," I whispered.

"He's a creepy guy," said Max, as he gave me his hand to help me up. "Come on, we better get back before he tells on us."

And we walked back on the path that led from the Elysian Field to the Women's Annex. The stars were all out by that time and Max pointed to Venus, which he knew, he said, because it was next to the crescent moon that night. It felt romantic and real being with him; and the notion of the two of us, artists with noble visions, somehow made the illusion of our new love all the stronger. Was it illusion this time? In this new place? In this place of illusory dreams come true?

It seemed like the theatre had just let out and we passed a few people with the same glow we'd had the night before. We reached the Women's Annex and waited a few minutes to be alone before kissing each other goodnight.

"Good night, Max. Thanks for rescuing me tonight."

"It's you who rescued me, so it was the least I could do. Good night. See you tomorrow." And he kissed me once more, gently, on my forehead.

What a warm feeling I had as I entered our room. My roommates were there, innocuous enough; friendly, yet quiet, which was perfect for my sense of privacy and space. The gong sounded soon after that and you could sense the lights going out one by one all over the Colony.

Outside my window, the moon was conjunct Venus...and I had a new man—so soon. Maybe it was real this time.

I fell asleep right away and was walking down a dark, mysterious path. Suddenly I saw this enormous, red truck coming straight at me— very fast. I was ready to start screaming—the truck was going to hit me...and I saw the driver—it was Geramund, grinning like the Devil as he sped my way, ready to run me over. But just as he was about to hit me, Max appeared and held up his hand at the truck. His erection showed through his trousers. He held up his hand and the truck stopped. It was the first time the truck had ever stopped. Max was able to stop it. He had the magic power. He had the power to stop the truck.

Geramund disappeared and the truck disintegrated into the air; and Max and I walked hand in hand toward the Elysian Field. Micky and Dave were there. It was good to see them. They were holding hands— how odd. We were all getting married. It was going to be a double wedding.

There was Hans—he was going to lead the ceremony. Erda was crying, wearing a white dress garlanded with daisies. Everyone was there. The music started: Wagner's *Lohengrin*. Max and I were naked. Micky and Dave wore tuxedoes. Hans and Erda had haloes over their heads.

And I woke up. Everyone was asleep. The Colony was dark and quiet. And I wasn't screaming; finally, I wasn't screaming. I felt at peace and looked forward to my next day at the Colony, the place where I learned to stop screaming...for a while.

CHAPTER SEVENTEEN: MICKY

What a night. It was like a dream come true. There Dave was in my bed. I had him. I had him where I wanted him: in my arms. I held his strong body, muscles and all; I held him, I embraced him, I kissed him on the back of his neck. His strength was my strength; and my strength was his. I felt his biceps, his ass, his stiff cock, his hair, which smelled like something sweet, something reminiscent of my past, which made me feel tender and warm.

I held him all night. We didn't really make love—it was better than that. We were closer than that. We were two men sleeping together—eager and strong, eager and warm, melting into each other. It felt like the best night of my life.

"Micky?" he asked much later, after we had slept a little.

"Yeah, man?" I said, kissing his neck with my arm around him.

"It feels good with you holding me, buddy. It feels good. Hold me like this as long as you want. I feel good with you."

How sublime it is, the way two men speak to each other in the night.

"Oh, baby, I feel good with you, too," I said, moving my hand down slowly from the top of his chest to his belly button and then his pubic hair and his dick, wet with excitement.

"Do me, will you?"

"Anytime, man," I said.

I rolled him over and he was even bigger than I remembered from the car. He ooooed and ahhhed and came real quick, especially for someone who'd had as much to drink as he had. I came with him, rubbing against his leg; and we lay there in a fountain of our own cum, happy, released, and completely free with each other.

I got up to get a towel but when I returned he was fast asleep. What a sight he was—he was golden…a pure, golden man—and he was all mine, at least for that night. That night I'll never forget. My night of nights. The night I had Dave in my bed, loving me, needing me, making me strong.

I dried us off and stroked his thick hair, thinking, This is a man. This is a perfect example of a man. My man, Dave.

I covered us up and put my arm around him. He said, real quietly, "Yeah, feels good."

I turned out the light and we lay there together in the dark, ready to fall asleep once more. But right before I fell asleep, I opened my eyes—and I could have sworn I saw this bluish-white, golden light surrounding him, making him glow like an angelic being, like an angel sent down just for me. I closed my eyes again, never having felt so good before.

And we drifted off like that, holding each other, until morning.

CHAPTER EIGHTEEN: RAVEN

Perhaps you humans are affected by the configuration of the stars in the sky, your weak and ever-striving natures making you susceptible to the cosmic forces above. But we cars are beyond all that nonsense; we are material beings and therefore immune to possible psychic influences, whether they exist or not.

Thus I was not affected by the lovely crescent moon and beautiful Venus in the sky last night, as I assumed my master and Dave were, as I imagined them having a splendid evening inside Micky's house. Yet what was for them, perhaps, a blissful night, turned out for me to be the worst night of my car life—and as you will see, possibly one of my last.

I am sure you have experienced being at one of your social gatherings with a person you positively could not stand. I am sure you have made the best of the situation; and probably avoided each other by staying on opposite ends of the gathering space. But can you imagine if you were forced to spend the entire night in the same bed with a person you considered to be deeply and utterly vile in every way?

This is the equivalent of what I underwent last night in the driveway next to that beastly and ungodly creature, that big red truck, whom I was forced to share my driveway with and whose presence, now, has nearly killed me.

For I am telling this account on top of a lift somewhere in a car hospital, what you humans call "The Shop"—and I tell it in complete physical agony. Please be aware that they do not have painkillers for cars. And if you find this idea amusing, I beg you to have some sensitivity at least for our hero, Micky, who may likely have to part from me, which would make him very unhappy—not to mention what it would do to me: the fate of having a new master, or worse, being sent to the Junkyard, where my current car life would end.

But I cannot think of such things at the moment. I am trying to get through this long night of torture. You humans have a term for it, but it does not apply to cars: The Dark Night of the Soul. Since we cars do not have souls, although we do have minds, it does not exist with us. But in a metaphorical sense, it is truly my Dark Night of the Soul; and I am trying to distract myself by conversing with you, because the pain is so great up here that I do not know if I can endure the night without your company.

What I have been through in the last twenty-four hours I would never wish on anyone, vehicle or human. I have experienced utter horror, utter disgust, utter degradation.

Naturally, the vulgar vehicle was thrilled to be shacking up with me all night and took the opportunity to share her fumes in the most contemptuous manner possible—by blowing them directly up my tailpipe, which was beyond rude, beyond anything I could have imagined. Not only did she contrive to do this; but totally against my will, forced me to know everything about her. I now know what she carries and why she carries it.

I cannot think too long on this subject, however, because if I do, I am afraid I will not be able to last the night. It is unthinkable, too dreadful to contemplate. It is the most terrifying thing in the world to be confronted with who you really are. How many people can look at themselves in the mirror? How many have the courage to face the truth about themselves? And what will it do to Micky if he ever finds out? Please do not force me to reveal it to you; I simply cannot take the responsibility at this time, for fear of losing my auto consciousness altogether.

What I have undergone is equivalent to a human heart attack and stroke combined. I do not know if there is any hope for me; and I believe it is up to my master to choose how much he wants to spend for my survival. Apparently, my transmission is completely shot and my battery equally dead; and Micky will have to pay for new ones in each case. And, to add insult to injury, he is at this very moment deciding whether to keep me or replace me.

Not only am I in pain, I am in anguish. This is the cruelest fate possible for a car as loyal as I.

Please forgive me if this story does not make perfect sense, as I am trying to be as coherent as possible under the circumstances, hoisted up on this lift. Allow me to now recount a few of the recent events:

In the morning, Micky came out to start me up, having discovered that he was out of tomatoes, wanting, I believe, to make Dave a tomato and Gruyère omelet. Micky always kept a generous supply of ripe, red tomatoes in his kitchen, I happened to know, because he told me once how good they were for his prostate gland, some organ that only male humans have. But when he tried to start me up, I was dead, of course, because of the circumstances I have begun to relate. He brought Dave outside to "give me a boost," as they called it; and they attached these electrical wires from that loathsome truck to me. They wanted to give me her electricity—which would definitely have killed me, had it worked.

But I refused the transfusion from her; I would not accept life from a vehicle of death. Which leads me to the rest of my story:

They had to call the tow truck, the car ambulance as it were, and hook me up to it and pull me all the way over here, which was an utterly humiliating experience, simply the worst in my car life. I am not a young car. I do not know if I can survive this torture—physical, mental and emotional. It is truly my Dark Night of the Soul.

As I said, the truck revealed everything to me, perhaps satisfying the curiosity I had previously, but telling me much more than I ever cared to know. She has nearly killed me, as she has killed many others. For she is surely a truck of death and destruction.

I hope you understand that I simply do not have the energy to articulate her mystery to you now. It would be better to contemplate for yourself what this mystery is and decide if you truly want to know it. I am able to say *this*, however, which is partly related to it: The biggest mystery of all is who we really are.

You humans live your lives so unaware of people, events, and their meanings, never stopping to look at the deeper truths, the profound realities. Only when you are near your deaths do you seem to ponder the higher meaning of life. But there are meanings to be found, and truths to be learned, and knowledge to be perceived in many unexpected ways. Ah, you humans are foolish: you utilize *our* technical brilliance to escape from thinking about your lives. The faster and further we can drive you—away from yourselves—the less you have to contemplate the true nature of your inner mind.

These are the thoughts I share with you from my deathbed as it were, this excruciating suspension in the air. It may give me a high perspective from which I look down upon the world; but it is, as I have said, by no means pleasant and by no means peaceful.

For we pay for the truths that we learn in this life, be we cars or humans; and we learn that the price we pay is worth every penny of its equivalent in time....

I have got to stop now; it is painful to talk, it is painful to think, it is painful to *be* at all. But first, I would like to ask of you one request, if I am no longer around to fulfill it myself:

Please watch over the children that I love: Micky, Dave, and Viagra—please watch over them if I am not able to do so. Will you do this for me? Will you honor the last request of a dying car?

For I love these children and I love what they stand for. Each of them wants to live on this earth in a way that is right for them, that is true for them. Will you follow their stories and support them? Will you be with them if I cannot be?

Will you listen to their voices and try, for once in your life, to...how shall I say...to achieve an understanding that is beyond yourself? Beyond your own life, your own opinions? For these children want big things. They are big children. They have big dreams.

Please listen to their voices and help them to go on.

PART THREE: ESCAPE

CHAPTER NINETEEN: VIOLET

"Show me a happy artist and I'll show you a merry mediocrity," said Geramund, peering over my shoulder in the Painting Shack two weeks later. I was trying to put the finishing touches on my painting, which was nearly done.

"Very clever, Geram," I replied, "but who's the happy artist? I never claimed to be."

"I never said you were, Violet. You just seem so happy here."

"Well, that's here. You don't know what my former life was like. Now stop peeking—I'm not ready to show this yet."

"Well as soon as you're ready, you let me know. I want to be the first to see it."

"I'm not promising anything. Come on, let me finish."

"OK, Violet. You win again."

"It's not a question of winning or losing. Why does everything have to be so competitive with you? Come on, grow up. Work on your own painting."

"Well, I never."

Then he finally left me alone.

In a way, he was right: I had experienced such happiness with Max in the last two weeks; and as I managed to gnaw away at the remnants of my pain, leaving an impression on the canvas that was cathartic while at the same time enlivening, I was able to enjoy life while experiencing a certain kind of death. I was finally able to release my childhood and discover a fulfilling adulthood—or so I thought at the time. Working on my painting in the day and seeing Max at night made me feel better than I had ever felt; and I thanked whatever gods or stars there were, for I knew that such perfection could hardly last forever. And I was right.

Who should enter the Painting Shack at that moment but Hans, the first time he visited since I began my work there.

"Hello, Hans," I said, "What brings you this way?"

"I came to see you, Violet. How are you?"

"To tell you the truth, I've never felt better. Working on this painting has allowed me to truly express myself—it's been incredible. Would you like to take a look? Don't let Geramund see. He wants to be the first. But I think you deserve the privilege."

"I would be honored. And I think Geramund would understand. Let me see what you've got there."

"It's not completely finished yet. But I'm starting to feel satisfied."

He gave my painting a long, hard look over and then he started to click his tongue, as if something were wrong.

"What's the matter?" I asked.

"What's the matter? Nothing, my dear. Finished or not, this is a disturbing work. And it's one of the most profound I have seen so far at the _____ Colony. You ought to be truly proud of yourself. Do you realize this?"

"I don't know; I'm not sure. Thank you, Hans. It's so good to hear this from you. I've painted it with all my heart. I've let it all out, so to speak."

"You have the potential to be a great painter, Violet, for your will is aimed at something great. Look at the way you choose to mix your colors—not in the conventional way, I assure you. Look at that little girl—look at that older man. I have rarely seen such a cacophony of color or drama in one painting since Goya; and frankly, my dear, I'm embarrassed to even pretend to know what to say. Seeing something like this makes my mission worth everything."

"Oh, Hans, I'm going to cry. Thank you. Thank you for having me here."

"No," he laughed, "it's me who is going to cry. I always thought you might have talent; but never imagined it could approach something of this magnitude. Do you think you could finish it by Thursday? We could include it in the next show. I am certain we could sell this for a

84

small fortune."

"Thursday...let me see...that's five days from now? I'm a little unaware of the days around here."

"That's right."

"Yes, I think I could do that. I'm sure I can."

"That's good. Now there was something I wanted to talk to you about."

"Oh, something else?"

"That's right."

"OK." I put down my brush and gave him my undivided attention.

"Violet, how shall I say this to you? We have a certain kind of reputation at the _____ Colony. It is our work that is important here; and we mustn't ever give the impression that we are a loose or wild place, but a serious place for serious work."

"What are you getting at?"

"There have been a few rumors, a few complaints actually, about the hours you have been keeping and the extra time you have been spending with Max. Some of the people who are not fortunate to have this kind of experience are perhaps a bit...envious?—and it doesn't bode well with the main function here, which is to produce the best work from everyone at all times. You have been missing breakfast, I've noticed; and I understand you have been arriving late here at the Painting Shack. So I'm afraid I have to ask that you stop seeing Max privately. Meals and social functions are fine, of course. But the rest will simply not do. It is not that kind of colony."

"Oh, Hans, please let me explain...."

"No need for that, Violet. We want to encourage greatness here. And I can see that greatness is something you are very close to achieving. It would be a shame if some romantic liaison were to spoil that. We simply could not permit that here."

"But I just wanted to—"

"Please try to understand. That is how it has got to be. Keep up the good work, Violet. I know that your painting will triumph in the next show. It could make you a name for yourself. Work hard now, my dear."

And he was gone.

I knew there was one person I had to see right away.

I turned my painting, covered it, washed my brushes and hands, and headed promptly toward the Sculpture Shop.

But when I got there, who should be talking to Max but Hans! I quickly turned around but Max's eyes met mine instantly—and Hans noticed it. He turned and saw me sneaking away.

I was discovered. Hans saw me trying to disobey him.

Suddenly my life had become complicated. I was no longer free. My happiness was severely threatened. And I was going to have to make a choice.

I returned to the Painting Shack to finish my painting as quickly as I could. I had no idea what I intended to do at that point except to complete my work and talk to Max at the soonest opportunity.

I was not about to live in a society where greatness and integrity were honored, yet forced. I was not about to be told how to behave.

And if freedom meant misery, I would have to be miserable once again.

CHAPTER TWENTY: VIOLET

The final gong had sounded a half hour ago. I waited by my window in the darkness for the light of Max's flashlight. We had quietly made our plan at dinner that night.

I waited but he didn't seem to be coming. God, if he didn't come, I didn't know how I'd get through the night! My roommates were sleeping soundly; and I was all dressed and ready to go.

Finally I saw the flicker of Max's flashlight. I quietly exited the Women's Annex and saw the full moon high in the sky. There was Max, his hair all black and wavy, this natural, talented man whom I loved.

"Hi!" he whispered. "Come this way."

We tiptoed together down a secret, alternative path we had discovered. You could hear the night crickets chirping and an occasional owl hooting. The sky was lit up with stars and the moon shone on our path, leading the way to the Elysian Field. The smell was that sweet summer scent, stored in the memory, a mixture of honeysuckle and herbs—practically an imagined smell, hidden away in memories like these.

Max's hand took mine as we headed toward the field. We didn't need to talk; we needed to be together, to make love once more, this time under the full moon. The danger of the outing made it quite an adventure—and I'll never forget the look on Max's face—that courageous, yet amused look—almost like Micky's—as he led me, bold and unafraid.

Finally we reached our favorite spot. We hadn't spoken more than two words. As if in a trance, we stripped off our clothes and gazed at each other, aroused in the moonlight. Our desire was so strong—and now that it was forbidden, it made the passion all the more intense.

We lay down in our favorite spot beneath the tall grass; and, as if in a hurry, for fear of being discovered, Max entered me almost right away. He filled me, making me feel whole, always reminding me a little of Dave, yet feeling unique and smelling sweeter, with the promise of great things from each other, great works of art with each other—our love, our art, our bodies, our souls.

"Oh, Violet!" he shouted. "I can't stand it. I can't stand it another minute!"

"Ah, Max, I'm right with you...."

And we screamed together in the field under the full moon. We screamed with all the joy we had; we exorcized anything that was ever sad in us. For I think we both knew that it would be our last time together.

As if out of consideration, almost, for the fulfillment of our lovemaking and the ensuing afterglow; as if it were planned that we should complete our last moments together under the moon and stars; as if some force allowed us the chance to share our love uninterrupted— without warning, a glaring spotlight suddenly shone on our naked bodies, frightening us back to reality.

We scrambled for our clothes; we scrambled for our decency. But it was too late: we were discovered. We couldn't see the faces behind the glare of the light at first. It was all very jarring.

Yet neither of us seemed surprised to find Hans and Geramund behind their torches of reality; neither of us seemed ashamed to be discovered, like Adam and Eve, in our nakedness. We slowly dressed and prepared ourselves for the worst.

"Max and Violet," Hans said calmly, "I will spare you the embarrassment of a lecture at the moment, my friends. Please meet me immediately following breakfast tomorrow morning in my office. Thank you. Good night."

Geramund said nothing, but I'll never forget the expression on his face; in fact, I intend to paint it someday, for it was an expression that told the story of an individual life: the gloating look of a man having won a temporary battle, knowing that he would ultimately lose, as he had always lost, the war of kindness and virtue.

For indeed it was a war to be waged, the war to be virtuous and kind in this world, when all about you, everywhere you looked, the meanness and baseness of people without talent or sensitivity would constantly threaten to drag you down into their pit of normalcy, of conformity, of safety.

Max and I walked silently back on the main path, feeling the serenity of lovers who knew that their time was upon them...and who lingered in the moment, cherishing the time they still had.

CHAPTER TWENTY-ONE: VIOLET

A strange glow seemed to hover over the dining room the next morning, like a cloud that had descended to shroud the emotions of all within its midst. No one seemed to be talking; everyone seemed to be looking in the direction of Max and me. It was a very uneasy feeling, as if the entire colony had been alerted to our wrong-doings.

Only the simplest of words were spoken:

"Could you pass the sugar, please?" I asked.

"Sure," he answered. "Get any sleep?"

"Not much."

"Me neither. I've got no appetite."

Silence.

I looked around the room but no one would make eye contact with me; as soon as my eyes met theirs, they would look away, like jurors who had determined my guilt.

"I'm getting out of here," I said. "I'll meet you outside the office."

"OK, Violet. I better stay for the moment."

There seemed to be quite a murmur when I rose from our table, but perhaps it was my imagination. Sometimes we feed our paranoia with the tiniest bit of evidence to convince ourselves that the world is against us.

I went to the restroom to wash up before our meeting and suddenly felt a wave of nausea. Oh great—was I going to be sick? But the feeling passed and I patted my face with cold water, preparing myself for the worst, which truly was to follow.

When I approached the door of the office, Max was just arriving. It reminded me of the time in third grade when I was sent to the principal's office. My cousin and I had been in the same class and were

90

continuously making each other laugh. I remembered how difficult it was to keep straight faces once we were inside the office, but somehow we managed. I didn't think that laughing with Max would be a problem to worry about today.

"You OK?" he asked.

"Not really," I said. "I'm expecting the worst."

"I don't know what to expect. This has never happened to me here."

Suddenly Hans stepped out the door and opened it for us to enter. "Please come in," he said.

We entered his office and he motioned for us to sit in the two chairs that were in front of his desk. Hans took the seat behind and began to talk:

"This is not a pleasant task that I need to perform this morning, but perform it I must, in order to maintain the dignity of our colony. Forgive me, Violet, for you have been very dear to me over the years, but I am afraid I will need to ask you to leave us. This is, of course, not easy for me to say, but you have deliberately disobeyed my wishes; and all the while I have been doing you the favor of letting you stay here. This is disturbing to me. I have discussed the matter with Erda and both of us think that your leaving is the only possible solution under the circumstances. Please take a day or two—no more—to finish the work on your painting. We will take it ourselves into town on Thursday and include it in the next show."

"And if you sell it...?" I asked, with a lump in my throat.

"Yes, we do expect to sell it."

"Well...." It was hard to get the words out. "How will I get reimbursed for my share? Or whatever I'm supposed to get for it?"

Max gave me a sympathetic look.

"My dear Violet," said Hans, "has no one explained to you the way it works here?"

"What do you mean?" I asked, on the verge of tears. "What do you mean, 'the way it works here?' "

"Apparently, my dear girl, you seem to be a little naïve, I assume from your innocent tone of voice. How do you suppose we support ourselves here at the _____ Colony? How do you suppose we can afford to offer you free room and board and a beautiful place to work? Have I asked you for a single penny since you have been here? The one thing I ask you for is dedication to your art. Which you have provided in a highly impressive manner. That is your payment to us, Violet. It is the art that we sell to support the function of our colony. I thought you understood this."

"Nobody explained this to me. Max!"

He opened his mouth but nothing seemed to come out of it.

"Max knows full well," Hans continued, "how things operate here and perhaps he should have explained it while you were so busy late at night. Your naïveté will get you into trouble in this world, Violet. I hope this will be a good lesson that will help you in the future. You are to finish your painting in the next day or two at the most. This is your payment to us. And then you are to leave."

"Hans," Max tried to interject.

"Max, we welcome you to stay if you continue to produce the work you have been producing. Violet, you are no longer welcome here. You will finish your painting and then you will leave us. Even if you don't do any more work on it, it is still quite saleable; and I'm sure that Geramund could put the final touches on it that would be required...."

"Don't you *dare* let Geramund touch my painting!" I shouted, surprising myself—and I was sure the two men as well. I found myself standing, feeling strong in the face of danger.

Hans rose to meet my gaze: "No need for that, my dear, if you finish it yourself. That is all I have to say to you. Max, you will stay for a moment. I want to have a few words with you in private. That will be all, Violet."

I just stood there; I just glared at him.

"Oh, and one more thing, my dear. As long as it's the time for learning lessons—especially lessons to instruct us on our naïveté, shall we say—it would be good for you to understand the effect that your beauty has on men and women in this world. It would be good for you to realize that it's not always a blessing to possess the beauty that you have. It stirs people up, both men and women...and it threatens to wreak havoc upon our society here. Do you understand me, Violet? I sincerely hope that you will leave our place and this experience with a little more self-knowledge than you had when you arrived."

"Oh, I've got self-knowledge, all right," I replied, trying to get my words out. "I've got self-knowledge...." But I couldn't seem to master any clever phrase or comeback; so holding back any tears that might have been welling up, I looked Max in the eyes and darted out of the office.

And then I did start crying. I didn't know where to go, but found myself walking as quickly as possible to the Painting Shack. Something told me I'd better check on my painting right away. I passed a few familiar faces but I didn't want to speak to anyone. I needed to make sure my painting was safe.

I entered the Painting Shack and couldn't believe what I saw. My painting was turned around, uncovered, and Geramund was staring at it. When he saw me, he gave me a big grin.

"Get away from my painting, Geramund!" I shouted. "How dare you touch it?"

"Violet, don't you worry, your painting is safe with me. Do you think I would ever harm a thing of such beauty? Of such genius?"

"You make me sick. You *are* sick, you know that? You've spoiled this whole experience for me. It's all your fault!" And I lunged toward him, wanting to destroy him, wanting to tear out the sickness, the evil that stood before me.

But he twisted my arms before I could ever reach his face: "Now, now, Violet...let's remain calm, shall we? Let's work together in peace, shall we?" He released my arms, forcing them to rest at my side.

"There, there. That's a good girl, that's a good painter. Let's finish your painting like a good girl, so that Hans can be proud of you. As proud of you as I am, Violet. I am so proud of you. So proud."

I slowly approached my painting while Geramund watched. My body was shaking. I picked up a fine brush and dipped it in black paint. Then I painted on the bottom right-hand corner in big, block letters:

THE BATH. And I said, "It's finished."

I dipped another brush into paint that was blood-red—and underneath the title, I painted...*Violet*. It was the most beautiful name I had ever seen.

CHAPTER TWENTY-TWO: DAVE

You know, it was fun staying at Micky's house—it really was—I mean it. And I enjoyed being with him, in bed and out of bed. I guess you could say we were having some kind of relationship, some kind of friendship—guys, you know?

I had no problem with that. And Micky was a funny character. He had all these red toy trucks and rocket ships all over the place—he said it was a collection that he had ever since he was a kid. And every once in a while, he would actually read my mind. Really! Like I'd be thinking about something, a waitress, say, who I'd just met at a diner—and he'd say, "Who's this girl named Alice with blond hair who's been on your mind?" Really! Just when I was thinking about her!

I was having a good time staying with Micky and everything—when I wasn't working, that is—but the one thing I wasn't getting was any... well, most guys would say, "pussy," but I'm not that crude, you know. Let's just say that I wasn't getting any female companionship. Which is what I liked. What I needed.

Micky helped me sort out the confusion in my mind—and that was great. But he was more like a friend, a good buddy. And the truth was, if you want to know, that hanging out with Micky was sort of a way to be close to his sister, who I was really starting to miss. And if I couldn't see her, Micky was the next-best thing.

Don't get me wrong. I never knew a guy like Micky. And I considered myself real fortunate to be able to know him. He taught me a lot of stuff. And I was always glad to learn new things. But I really missed Viagra and wished I could have figured out a way to find her.

Also, something that was getting to be a little bit of a drag—not too bad, just a little bit, you know, like maybe I could've found something better to do—was that I had to drive Micky everywhere when I was there, in between my driving gigs—which meant a lot of driving!—because his car was in the shop and he didn't have any way to get around.

So it was up to me to play chauffeur with Micky, which I didn't mind that much. But usually when I got to his house after a few hours of driving, the last thing I wanted to do was go to the supermarket to pick up some tomatoes or something—even if it was to make me lasagna for dinner. Micky was a great cook. He was good at a lot of things. In fact, I can't think of anything he wasn't good at. A jack-of-all-trades, I guess that's what he was. And he never made me feel bad for not knowing something or anything. He made me feel smarter just being with him. I guess he liked me a lot.

But as I was saying, I missed Viagra. It'd been about a month since I'd seen her. So one day I asked Micky if there was any way we might track her down.

"Hey Mick, man," I said, "you know I'm happy to be hanging out with you. But the truth is, I really miss your sister. (I didn't want to lead him on or anything. I wanted to be totally up-front with him, you know?) Is there any way at all you think we could find her? I feel a little guilty about her leaving, cause in a way, I think it was partly my fault."

"Dave," Micky said, "nothing is ever your fault or not your fault. Things happen the way they're meant to happen. We learn from what happens to us. But I was thinking of something similar recently; and I do have one idea of how we might locate her. Let me try calling this friend of hers at work. Maybe, just maybe, she would know."

"Sounds like it's worth a try," I said.

So Micky picked up the phone and dialed. "Hello," he said, "May I speak to Frieda, please?" He covered the phone and said to me, "They're getting her."

"Frieda? Hi, this is Micky, Viagra's brother.... Yeah, we met once before at that Christmas party you had there.... Yeah, I'm good. How about you? Oh really? Oh, that's too bad. Is there something you can give the dog? Or something to put on your hand? Ah, that's good. Is the dog's name Sam? No, I didn't know that. It just came to me. Really!

I never knew the dog's name. No really, these things come to me every now and then. Yeah. Viagra told you? No, she was serious, she really was.

"Listen, I've got a friend here and the reason I'm calling is to see if you have any idea where Viagra might have gone. We're missing her and we're worried about her. It's been a couple of weeks.... Oh...well, it's worth a try...hang on.... Dave, could you hand me that pen? She's going to look up this number; she's got an idea. Frieda? Yeah, ready. Shoot. 581-408-7841. Great. I'll give it a try. Thank you so much, Frieda. Hope that you and Sam will get along better. Try giving him some French fries—yeah, I know—he likes them, ha-hah. Good talking to you too. Bye."

"Where is she? Does Frieda know?"

"She's not sure, but there's this guy who used to work there who opened up some sort of artists' colony and she thinks that Viagra might have gone there. It's worth a shot. Do you want to call?"

"Sure," I said. My ears felt like they were getting red. I felt like I was getting all excited, just thinking about talking to Viagra. I must have missed her more than I thought.

Micky gave me the number and I dialed it. I wondered how far away it was—I didn't recognize the area code.

A woman answered the phone. "Hello, this is the Colony. Jandice speaking. How can I help?" She sounded like she was from England or something.

"Oh hi. I'm trying to locate someone, but I'm not sure if they're there or not. Is there a woman named Viagra there?"

"I don't know anyone by that name; will you hold a moment, please?"

"Sure.... She's put me on hold," I said to Micky.

After a few minutes, a German man came on the line.

"Who is this, please?" he asked, like he was really annoyed.

"Hi, my name is Dave and I'm trying to locate my friend, Viagra. Do you know if she's there, by any chance?"

"How did you get this number?"

"Through a friend of hers at work. Is there some problem? Is Viagra there?"

"She is staying here at the moment—but not for much longer. She should be leaving in a day or so. She is not allowed to receive calls here."

"Oh, well, could you give her a message then?"

"I suppose I could do that. What is the message?"

"Would you tell her Dave called? And that he looks forward to seeing her soon?"

"I will tell her that. Anything else I can help you with?"

"No, that's it. Thanks."

"Goodbye. And please do not call here again."

"I won't. Just give her the message, OK?"

"I will. Goodbye."

"Goodbye."

"Well?" Micky asked.

"That was strange."

"How so?"

"This guy was really nasty. But she's there and he says he'll give her the message. He says she's leaving in a day or so. Hopefully, she's coming home."

"Yeah, hopefully," he said.

Then Micky got a weird look on his face, like he saw something scary, but there was nothing scary around.

"What's the matter?" I asked him.

"Hard to explain," he said.

"Huh?"

"Don't want to scare you, Dave, but I get the feeling that Viagra's in some really bad danger. Like she's trapped somewhere and has to escape. Like she's got to steal something and get out of there. I don't know, it's just what I feel, it's just what came to me."

"How do you do this stuff?" I asked.

"It comes from being ultra-sensitive, from training my mind."

"Wow. You're a cool person to know, Mick. Glad you're my buddy. What am I thinking now?"

"You're thinking that I need to take care of you right away."

"Wrong! I'm thinking that I'm ready for that lasagna. I'm starved."

"OK, man. Let me get it ready."

He made off to the kitchen and I was left with the telephone number in my lap. I called the operator to find out where the area code was. But she told me there was no such area code. I said there had to be, that I just called there. She said, impossible. I said again that I just called. She said, "Sir, that's impossible. That area code doesn't exist."

I said, "Well, how do you explain that I just spoke to two people there?"

"Maybe you dialed the wrong number and thought it was that number."

"Oh…. Well, I suppose that's possible. I'll try the number again and check. Thanks a lot."

I clicked the receiver and dialed 581-408-7841.

"Hello, this is the Colony. Jandice speaking. How can I help?"

I tried to disguise my voice a little: "Hello, can you tell me what part of the US you're located in, please?"

"Who is calling?"

"I'm a driver and I have to make a delivery. Just wanted to plan my driving time a little."

"What are you delivering to us, sir?"

"I don't know, actually, ma'am. I never know what I'm delivering. I just deliver it. What part of the country are you in?"

"We're not in your country. Is this the same man who called before?"

"No, honey, I'm just trying to find out this information."

"Well, we're not in your country. And I suggest that you don't try to find us. We're pretty far off the map. Thank you."

And she hung up. This left me with a real queasy feeling, a real queasy feeling. Now I was *really* worried about Viagra. And I was going to have to go and find her.

CHAPTER TWENTY-THREE: MICKY

There was no talking him out of it.

And to tell you the truth, I respected him for that. When a man makes up his mind, if he really makes up his mind, there's nothing you can do to interfere. It has to do with his will: the test of a man's character, like his handshake. And Dave had a strong handshake, believe me. You could melt inside his handshake. You had to have a strong will yourself to shake hands with him.

And I did. But a strong will doesn't mean interfering with someone else's will—and his will was to go find Viagra, no matter how ridiculous the idea might have been. And it was not my place to go interfering with that. Of course, I tried at first to convince him how unrealistic it was that he would ever find her; but there was no deterring him.

And this proved to me what I suspected all along: that Dave really loved Viagra. I mean *really* loved her. And you know what? I was glad. I loved Dave, but if he was in love with my sister, at least it was all in the family. And when you love someone, you never want to interfere with what they need to do—even when that includes loving someone else.

So I tried to help him in every way I could to get started on his journey, which would begin that evening. I even called Frieda again—and I just caught her. I told her about Dave's call and the whole area code thing. But Frieda knew nothing about the location except that it was somewhere seven hours north of us. She thought it was in the United States, was pretty sure it wasn't in Canada, and remembered some strange conversation with the guy, Hans, right before he left. She thought he was joking, but he said something about the place being off the map, not in any real country—being in a special location, something like that. She didn't pay that much attention because she thought he was speaking metaphorically. But right before we said goodbye, she said:

"Wait a minute, Micky. I just remembered something. I almost forgot but I remember it now. He said that where he was going was off some road or highway number twenty-two. I distinctly remember the number twenty-two being in there because he said something about the number's mystical significance—but I thought he was joking, so I didn't pay that much attention."

"Frieda," I said. "Thanks a lot. This just might help my friend on his wild-goose chase. You have a good night now. Thanks again."

"Bye, Micky, take care of yourself."

"Dave," I said, "listen to this." He was pouring the wine for our lasagna. "Frieda thinks she remembers that the place is off of a Route 22 or some road like that. But definitely the number 22. About seven hours north of here. Maybe that'll help."

"Aw, thanks, Mick," he said.

He was always calling me Mick, which I liked, coming from him.

"You're a great guy, helping me like this. I know you don't want me to go, but it's something I've got to do. It's something I feel so strongly. I've got to find her. I don't care what she is or what they call her. I love her. I love you too, in a different kind of way—but I know I love her—can't explain it. I've got to find her."

So we sat down for our "last supper"—and it really was our last supper. Because after that evening, I would see him only one more time. But I didn't know that yet. There's so much I didn't know yet.

We all think we know a lot, but we really know nothing. None of us knows the twists and turns that life will take. We think we're in control—or we think we're powerless. But the truth is, we're neither. Life is going to hit you, whether you're prepared for it or not, with a big roller coaster snowball that comes crashing at you from the lightning clouds in the sky. Nothing you can do about it. So don't pretend to be smarter than the roller coaster snowball. Best thing to do is be ready for it. At least maybe you can catch it with your roller coaster mittens, the ones that grasp the bar in front of you as you hold on for dear life.

We gorged ourselves on lasagna and red wine, as if there were no tomorrow. For in a way, there *was* no tomorrow—only that evening—our last evening together. My buddy Dave and me, getting ready for the roller coaster snowball—that was about to hit all of us real, real hard.

CHAPTER TWENTY-FOUR: VIOLET

"Violet!" cried Arnie, late that afternoon as I was walking to my car. "Are you OK?"

"Thanks for asking," I said, running over to meet him on the road. "You seem to be the only one who's speaking to me, besides Max, that it."

"What did I tell you, Violet? The rumors are flying. They say you've been kicked out. Is it true?"

"Yes, very true. And everything seems so hypocritical to me now in a place that's supposed to have integrity. Why am I, the woman, being kicked out? Why weren't a number of things explained to me?"

"What things?"

"Like what happens to our art and who gets the money. Like love affairs being forbidden."

"They're not exactly forbidden, hun, they just have to be discreet—and not cross Geramund's path, I guess. He must secretly have a thing for you."

"He must secretly have a thing against humanity. I knew he would be my nemesis."

"What did I tell you?"

"Arnie, will you walk me to my car? I want to check the gas and tires. I think I'm leaving tomorrow."

"Tomorrow? I'm going to miss you, Violet. And I hardly even know you yet."

"Well, apparently, I'm too beautiful—Hans's words—to remain here. Isn't that disgusting? And it's the man who gets to stay—because of the money he gets for his work, I suppose."

"That's the world we live in. Not too different from *The Madwoman of Chaillot*—even here. Money is king. True art is what sells."

"What a wake-up call. It really irks me how a society or group can pretend to have integrity—to hold it higher than anything—and then twists its meaning to suit its purpose. I guess that's why I've avoided groups before. The group always wins out over the individual. The herd instinct always prevails. That's why groups are dangerous, whatever their philosophy is: you always end up having to do things their way. What's wrong with having a love affair if I'm doing good work? What's wrong with arriving a little late if I accomplish more than most people do anyway?"

"You're preaching to the choir, kid, I'm on your side."

"Here's my car. Look—there's something under the windshield wiper. I wonder what it could be." I unfolded the piece of paper and read it out loud to Arnie:

"Dearest Violet, we've got to act fast. Don't sit with me at dinner tonight. Get as much packed and ready as you can before the final gong. Just tell them you're getting ready to leave tomorrow, as instructed. Below is the number and address of my former dealer, about five hours away from here. If all goes well, I will call him tomorrow and tell him that you will be there with your painting. I know he will take you on. Meet me exactly one hour after the final gong tonight outside your door. Be ready to go. Have your car ready, but leave it in the parking lot. Fingers crossed! All my love, Max.

"Oh Arnie, this is a total surprise to me. You won't tell anyone, will you?"

"Course not, Violet. Max is an incredible guy. Careful—put the note away—Hans is coming."

"Oh my God."

"Hello, Arnie, Violet," he said in that contemptuously polite way of his. "May I have a word with Violet alone please?"

"Sure. See you later, Violet."

"Bye, Arnie. I'll look for you at dinner."

"Violet, I'm glad to run into you here. You had a call this afternoon from a Dave person. How did he get our number? Did you tell someone you were coming here?"

"Of course not. I would never violate what we agreed on before I

104

arrived. But I don't think it's fair that once I'm here, you forbid me to see a man—or anyone—when I choose to. I am a free woman, an adult; and if my work is not suffering, then I don't see the harm. I don't appreciate the way I've been treated as a woman. The painting is finished—and I'll be leaving early tomorrow morning."

I walked away from him before he could answer me, the note safely tucked away near my heart.

What a long evening it was. Dinner was pleasant enough with Arnie, but of course we couldn't talk about anything meaningful with everyone staring and whispering. Max caught my eye several times, winking each time—and once I was bold enough to pucker my lips and send him a kiss, which he responded to with his fingers crossed in the air.

After dinner, I brought my car around to the Women's Annex and started loading up. Trying to act naturally, I explained to my roommates that I would be leaving the next morning after breakfast. They didn't seem especially sorry to see me go, perhaps because they knew they would sleep better without my late-night comings and goings.

My packing complete, I drove back to the parking lot and took a little walk around the Colony before going to bed. I was free to walk around by myself, wasn't I? I passed by all the art shops, I passed by the gong, the theatre—and realized how much I would miss this place. This magic place that held so much promise for me, so much freedom.

But we learn from our experiences, I thought, as I headed back to my bunk for the final time; and I was ready to move on to the next phase of my life, the next adventure, not knowing, of course, what could possibly be in store.

Dave called, I thought. How did I feel about that? How did he discover I was here? Would I be seeing him again? Would I ever see Max again? I realized that these were questions I couldn't answer that night.

And as I look back on it, I know it was best that I couldn't answer them then. Life teaches us when we're ready for its lessons; though sometimes the lessons seem overwhelming when they occur.

I snuck into bed with my clothes still on, my bag and my keys just beside me, ready for my clandestine escape. The final gong sounded with its nightly promise of inspiring dreams: dreams of art, dreams of greatness—its chimes resounding in that secret place inside us, the place where we know we are destined for something great.

I lay there for one of the longest hours of my life, awaiting Max with his fire eyes—who would release me into the world once more.

CHAPTER TWENTY-FIVE: DAVE

Why did I have all that red wine? It was so good, it was hard to stop drinking it. And Micky was such a...what's that word? Conna Sir? Something like that...so he always had real good wine to go with whatever he was making. It was a lasagna to die for, I'll tell you. And we finished it off with his great coffee and chocolate brownies. I don't mean to make your mouth water, but it was enough to fuel me up for the road.

Ah, the road. What I really love the best, I think. I'm a true driver at heart. Nothing can thrill me more than a seven-hour night trip to nowhere. A night adventure to the Great Beyond. You never know what you might find on your journey—you can stop to gas up and all the night drivers live in that special night world, high on night driving, with a language and a look in their eyes all their own.

I knew this look, cause I had it, I felt it—I saw the other end of that look from behind my eyes. It was the look of adventure, of searching for the dream at the end of the drive, the reward waiting for you at the end of the tunnel. But it wasn't the reward, the destination, so much as the driving itself—the music, the thinking, the flying, going after something...who knows what? That feeling of freedom that no one can explain.

I was never happier than when I was on the road.

Except maybe when I was with Viagra. That's why I was going to find her. Hey, I was no fool—I knew what my chances were. But the thought of going after my dream of love, now that I knew what it was, now that I found it, was worth more to me than anything. And if it would take seven hours to get there or nowhere or somewhere, I didn't care. I was happy again.

Course, it was a little sad to leave Micky who I liked a lot and who I knew liked me more than a lot—and if I ended up finding his sister, what would that do to us as buddies? Hopefully make us closer, I thought.

I was going north and it was getting dark and I was feeling like everything was possible, like I believed in myself, like I could have any dream I picked—as long as I was willing to drive after it long enough and far enough. Hey, I was a dream Conna Sir! Yes, sir. I knew a lot about driving after a dream, even if that dream was to keep driving until you figured out what you wanted to find. Do you get me?

I realize I'm kind of talking in circles. But life and driving take you in circles. You go north, you go west, and you circle around and come back south. You hitch up for the night and then you start up again the next day. Always on the move, always going after that dream which doesn't go away, as long as you keep driving toward it. Does that make any sense?

Anyway, I guess you can tell, I guess you know by now that Viagra was my dream—and I would've driven more than seven hours to find her. Hey, I drove twelve hours non-stop in my day for nothing. So I would've driven twice that if I knew I could find Viagra. She was definitely a woman to find.

So I drove practically straight up 99 and then I turned off on 102, just cause I felt like it—and took 102 straight up almost all the way. Mick Jagger was on the radio, which made me think of Micky—then the Beatles—then Nirvana—then...I changed the station...and they were playing this woodland symphony type thing. It was nice, going to where I was going. Made me feel very woodland-like, you know? All pine trees and stuff.

Ah, I was feeling good, feeling like I might see Viagra soon, and feeling like I was sure I would—sure as hell, you know?

But, making a long story short, after pulling over once for some coffee and a piss, about an hour after that, I suddenly started getting real tired. I didn't want to get tired or anything. I wanted to get where I was going by that night, definitely—and maybe find Viagra the next day. So I forced myself to drive a little farther.

And then I saw it. I passed it, actually, and had to turn around. Route 22. There it was. I did a U-turn and backtracked a little and tried to feel out whether I should turn left or right onto it. I felt like it should be right, cause I really didn't know where the hell I was going—and as I said, I was getting tired. It was late—way after one in the morning by that time. Not that that was too late for me usually, but like I said, I shouldn't have drunk all that wine.

I went a ways on 22—it was west—and saw this road inlay thing, what do you call it? I pulled in there and decided to snooze until morning. I had made real good progress for the night, after all. And the next day I would find Viagra, wherever she was. I had that number and I'd figure something out.

So with good thoughts on my mind and a smile on my face, I conked out in my truck and started dreaming right away. Guess who I dreamed about? You got it. My dream girl, who else? We were driving together in my truck. She was taking a long trip with me. We were going after the same dream, which was to get nowhere, nowhere at all except the drive itself, you know?

We just drove and drove—we took turns—and I let her drive my truck. Boy, was she a pro! She knew how to drive it without any training. In fact, at one point, she drove us off the ground and we were flying in the air. Flying, dreaming, going after our dream together, which was to never really get there, just to enjoy the ride. What a happy dream. The two of us were real happy, real free.

We came down from the sky and suddenly I was watching the two of us, like a movie. I saw the truck going down Route 22...and it drove way off into the distance...and I saw THE END written on the screen... and I woke up on the real Route 22.

I was all fuzzy and hazy and wasn't sure if I was still dreaming or not, but I heard a whir of a car engine coming down a hill. It was kind of loud all of a sudden in a place that was mostly quiet and deserted, you know? I saw this car coming down this hill up a ways, and it was a white car, like Viagra's. It looked just like Viagra's car, like her Saturn, if I remembered right—only it had something big that it was carrying on top, all tied up on the roof rack, it looked like.

I figured I must still be dreaming, that I just wanted to see Viagra so much, I must still be dreaming...but the car drove slowly by me, very slowly...like it didn't know where it was going...like it was looking for me...like it wanted to see who I was, sleeping and dreaming inside my truck.

But after it passed me, it picked up speed and sped on down the highway real fast, like it was going somewhere important, somewhere in the important world—not like our dream road that went on forever. Couldn't have been Viagra, could it have? I knew I was still dreaming anyway, that I just enjoyed pretending it might be Viagra in her car and all.

I locked my doors, just in case, and lay down on my seat for a good night's sleep until the morning sun would wake me...and I'd go climb some hill and find Viagra...and take her off with me on the road once more...just the two of us...driving on the road....

CHAPTER TWENTY-SIX: VIOLET

Max was right on time.

"Hi!" I whispered. "You made it."

"So did you," he grinned.

He was carrying a large plastic bag with a bundle of cord under his arm.

"What's all that?" I asked.

"Packing stuff. You're lucky I have experience packing up my sculptures. This ought to be a cinch in comparison."

We started walking to the Painting Shack.

"What about Hans? What about Geramund?"

"We can pretty much relax about them—and hopefully this will be a breeze. No way is Hans going to be up this late two nights in a row—especially without Geramund."

"What do you mean? It's Geramund I'm worried about. What if he's guarding the Shack?"

"It's all been taken care of, sweetheart. That Arnie is a good friend of yours. After you read him my note, he came right over to see if there was any way he could help. So we devised this plan: Arnie is playing decoy. You see, Violet, you may have enemies, but you also have friends."

"What's Arnie doing?"

"Shhh...we have to be very quiet here...this is where Grego sleeps, near the gong. I hear he's a light sleeper, ringing the gong and all, so any noise might provoke him to come outside."

"OK," I said softly.

We tiptoed past the gong and toward the art shops. It was mostly all dark, except for the light of Max's flashlight.

Finally Max said, "I think we're pretty safe now."

"So what's the plan? What is Arnie doing?"

"We're lucky he's such a good actor. But this will probably be easy for him. It's pretty well-known here that Arnie is bipolar. He's been OK, on his medication and everything. But tonight—hopefully right now—he's feigning a manic episode in Geramund's room. He's going to keep Geramund occupied for a good hour. So we have an hour, which is more than enough time to secure your painting and for you to get out of here."

"Oh, Max. This is so scary. It's like being in an escape movie."

"I know, but it's real life. I'm your hero."

"You certainly are!" I leaned over and gave him a big kiss on the cheek.

"Hey, no romance tonight. I'm Harrison Ford and I've got to get you and your painting out of here. Hopefully this will all run smoothly."

We arrived at the Painting Shack. The smell was the same, but it was eerie seeing it completely dark, with Max's flashlight flickering as we opened the door.

"Now I want you to help me," he said. "Let's keep your covering on the painting and slide it into this bag."

It wasn't as difficult as it looked. Not all that cumbersome, the painting was relatively light for its size.

My heart was racing but Max seemed to be an expert at this. I kept watching the door, fearful that someone might enter, but it seemed like we were going to be OK.

"There we go," he said. "That wasn't too bad. Now I'm going to zip this up and get the cords ready. Violet, here's my spare flashlight. Take the road outside and quietly get your car. Bring it over this way. Leave it on the road. By the time you get here, I'll be all set. We'll carry your painting to the car, get it tied up—and since we're at the end of the Colony here, you'll be all ready to drive down the hill. Hurry, but be quiet!"

"OK, Max," I said. I tried to look confident, but I was terrified. What if we got caught?

"Oh, one more thing, Violet. Remember, you have every right to be doing this. This is your work. You own it. You never entered any agreement with Hans. Hurry up, now."

"OK."

I walked on the road, which was near the Shack, to the parking lot. I fumbled for my keys in my bag. Where were they? I couldn't find them. Oh my God. I looked and looked as I walked. Did I leave them at the Women's Annex? How could I be so stupid? They had to be there next to my bed. I thought I had put them inside my bag. So I made a quick detour to get my keys, which were hopefully there on the floor.

I was moving very quickly, trying to make up for lost time, but when I got to the Women's Annex, who should be sitting on the steps out front but one of my roommates, Robin, smoking a cigarette. Great, just what I needed.

"Oh hi, Robin, what are you doing up at this hour?"

"Couldn't sleep. I thought you were leaving tomorrow. Having one last fling before you go?"

"Not exactly—I mean, sort of. I forgot something. Excuse me."

I walked around her on the steps, entered our room, and sure enough, there were the keys on the floor by my bed. How could I be so careless? I quickly made my way out, passed Robin and said, "Get some sleep, now. It's going to be an exciting day tomorrow." I don't know what possessed me to say that.

"Exciting? How so?"

"You'll see...I've got to dash...bye!"

"Have fun," she said.

Now I ran to the parking lot. I couldn't believe I could be so stupid. OK, stop beating yourself up, I thought. Everything's going to be all right.

I got to my car and my hands were shaking as I unlocked it. I got in, started it up and tried to drive slowly and quietly toward the Painting Shack, which was in the same direction as the exit to the Colony.

It's funny how the Colony lost all of its beauty and magic that night; the only thing that existed was the task at hand: to get the painting and get out of there.

I arrived near the Painting Shack and left my car on the road. Max was there and the painting was all tied up and ready to go. I hoped it wouldn't get damaged during the drive.

"OK, honey," he said. "Very good. Just help me with this. That's it. Easy, right?"

I couldn't believe we were doing this. And how smoothly it was going, despite my mistake. We approached my car with the painting and Max had us flip it over so that it was facing up. We hoisted it on top of the rack up there—it was lucky I had one. And Max expertly tied it down.

"Now Violet, we shouldn't waste much time with goodbyes."

"Oh, Max."

"Pay extra attention when you're driving—remember, the painting is wider than your car, so don't drive too close to anything."

"All right."

He put his hands on my shoulders. "Listen to me. You are stealing your own painting. It's your own work. You have every right to be doing this. There is nothing unethical about it."

"Thank you for everything. I don't know how to thank you...."

"Shhh...don't worry about that now. You've got the address and directions to my dealer. I'll be calling him first thing in the morning. Go straight there. You're a great painter, Violet. Don't you ever forget that."

"Will I ever see you again?"

"I've got to stay here, honey. This is my home. I'm happy here. Your place is in the world. To make a name for yourself. It's your birthright. You better go before someone comes."

And we hugged each other for the last time.

"Oh, before I forget. Here's a little something to remember me by." He reached into his pocket and pulled out a small object, wrapped in blue tissue paper. "Quickly, now, Violet...I want you to have this. It's a sculpture of you, my darling. You're my muse, my inspiration. Don't you ever forget it."

"Max...."

"Go!" he commanded, like a smiling sergeant in love with his soldier.

"Aye, aye, captain," I said, getting the sniffles.

I entered the car and started the engine. I looked out my window one more time at Max, and will always remember his godlike, fiery gaze as he said to me, "Don't look back—keep going."

He turned around and left me there, his sculpture in my hand, as I began my journey down the hill. I passed the large rock at the beginning of my descent. There was a message on it facing me in big, white letters:

You are leaving the _____ Colony. Have you accomplished what you set out to achieve?

"Yes," I answered out loud, "Yes, I have. I am bringing my painting into the world."

I drove around the rock and started the steep descent to the road below. My heart was still beating rapidly; and between the fear, the excitement and the sadness of leaving Max, it was difficult to know my true feelings about anything—except concentrating on the drive and making it down safely, as the gravel churned in my wheels.

Finally I reached the bottom of the hill; and feeling completely dazed, in a different world altogether, I couldn't remember whether to turn left or right. I had to use Max's flashlight—I had forgotten to return it—and look at the directions. They said to turn right so I did.

It felt like I was dreaming only I was awake. But I couldn't decide if it was a good dream or a bad dream, an idyllic dream or a nightmare. I started driving east very slowly and suddenly I thought I might be hallucinating: I was sure I saw the red truck of my nightmares. It was pulled over on the other side of the road, sitting there in this cul-de-sac, as if it were waiting for me.

I couldn't see any driver in it; and it didn't threaten me much since it wasn't coming at me. It was just sitting there. As I slowly drove by it, though, I realized for the first time that the scary truck from my dreams looked just like Dave's truck. He had the same truck that was in my nightmares!

What a strange realization this was. I wondered about its meaning in my life, knowing that it wasn't the best time to figure it out.

I looked straight at the truck. I passed it calmly, taking in my realization, trying to learn something from it, as if I had conquered, perhaps, my fear of it. I thought of my childhood, I thought of Micky and Dave and Max; I even thought of my father—and I was ready to travel beyond them all.

I took a deep breath, feeling like a new woman again, remembering that I had given birth to a work of art. With my painting securely fastened to the roof above me, I felt a new kind of dignity, a new kind of strength; and I said goodbye to the red truck, as I sped down the highway toward Max's dealer, five hours away, where I would arrive very early the next morning.

CHAPTER TWENTY-SEVEN: MICKY

I was feeling so lonely after Dave left. I had no boyfriend, no girlfriend, no sister—and perhaps worst of all—no car. I had to call the next day to see what the story was with poor ol' Rave.

But there was one thing I did have: my laptop. I decided to sit down right then and there and write something. I immediately got inspired: I would write a children's book. I knew I could do it. And the title came to me right away: THE BIG RED TRUCK. I liked it. It didn't have to be too long; there would be plenty of illustrations. And I wanted it to be scary. Were children's books allowed to be scary? Well, this one was going to be for sure.

I decided not to waste any time and to sit down and write the book immediately.

THE BIG RED TRUCK

Once upon a time, a very long time ago, but not *too* long ago, there lived a brother, a sister, and a big red truck. The truck was so big and made so much noise when it drove down the street, that all the children who lived on the block were afraid of it.

The driver of the truck was a real nice guy, but he couldn't understand why all the children were so afraid of his truck.

One day, he parked the truck in front of the brother and sister's house. The brother's name was Mikey and the sister's name was Veronica. He walked up the path to their house and rang the bell.

He was happy when he saw Mikey and Veronica at the door together.

"Hello," said the driver of the truck. "My name is Dan. What are your names?"

Veronica said, "This is Mikey."

And Mikey said, "This is Veronica."

"Who are you?" asked Veronica. She liked the man at the door because he had a friendly smile and was very good-looking.

"My name is Dan and I drive that big red truck outside."

"Oh," said Mikey. "The big red truck. We know that truck. All the kids are afraid of it."

"I know," said Dan, "that's why I'm here. I wanted to ask you why? Why are all the children afraid of my truck? It's so big and long and has such a pretty color."

"But it makes such a loud noise!" exclaimed Veronica.

"I know," admitted Dan, "but that's what big trucks do. Is your Mommy or Daddy home? Maybe they would know."

"No," said Mikey. "They're not home. We don't know where they are. We've been waiting for them to come home for a long, long time."

"Oh, I see," said Dan. "Well, would you like to go for a ride? *You're* not afraid of my truck, are you?"

"No, we're not afraid," said Veronica. "We're not afraid of anything. But we think we should wait for our parents to come home first and then ask them."

"Oh, OK," said Dan. "But I think it would be a lot of fun. And then you could show the other kids that there's nothing to be afraid of."

"I'm not so sure that there's nothing to be afraid of," said Mikey, looking very smart all of a sudden.

"What do you mean?" asked Dan, with a great look of bewilderment on his face.

"Well," replied Mikey, "your truck is very big and very long and our block is very small. What do you carry in back there, anyway?"

"I can't tell you that," said Dan.

"Why not?" asked Veronica.

"Because I'm not allowed."

"What do you mean, 'you're not allowed?' " she asked again.

"Just what I said. I'm not allowed to tell nice little kids like you what I carry in my truck."

"But why not???" they both asked at once.

"Because I don't *know* what I carry in back of my truck!" laughed Dan.

"You don't know?" asked Mikey.

"You don't know?" asked Veronica.

"No, I don't know—do you want to come look and find out?"

"Mikey and I need to discuss this in private a minute, OK?"

"OK, Veronica. I'm in no rush," said Dan.

The brother and sister whispered in each other's ears back and forth for a minute or two. Then Mikey walked toward the front door very bravely and said to the truck driver, Dan:

"OK, Dan, we'll come see what's in back of your truck—if you really don't know what's back there."

"Oh, I don't know," said Dan, "and I never lie."

"OK, then," said Mikey, taking his sister's hand.

They walked down the path from their house to where the truck was. All the other little kids were scared and were watching from their windows.

Dan and Mikey and Veronica walked slowly toward the back of the truck. Dan moved the heavy bar that was keeping the back locked up. And he started to open the back of the truck as the brother and sister watched, while the other children watched them to see their reaction.

Dan opened the truck and the children looked into it for a few minutes without saying anything. Then all of a sudden, they both started to scream. They screamed and screamed and screamed—and the whole neighborhood could hear it.

They ran back very quickly up the path to their house and immediately locked the front door once they were inside. Then they ran to the back door and locked that one, too. Then they ran upstairs to their bedrooms and closed their doors, locking the doors behind them.

Then they both got under their beds and hid there, shaking.

The doorbell rang.

Silence.

The doorbell rang again.

Silence.

The doorbell rang once more.

Nobody moved.

Silence.

More silence.

Then Mikey and Veronica heard the sound of the front door being unlocked—and they could hear somebody coming up the stairs. They each shook underneath their beds—and wished that they were with each other during such a scary time.

They heard the footsteps coming up the stairs. Slowly, slowly, slowly coming up the stairs. Which room would the person go to first? Mikey's or Veronica's?

Both Mikey and Veronica were trying real hard not to scream. They were holding their screams in. It was the scariest time they ever had in their lives.

Suddenly both of their doors flew open—even though they were locked! Somebody had the keys!

But they realized as they shook there under their beds, that everything was going to be OK, because their Mommy and Daddy had come back home and had presents to give them.

They were so relieved! And they hugged and kissed their Mommy and Daddy—they were so glad to see them. And they told them the story of the big red truck. And the truck driver named Dan.

But their Mommy and Daddy told them never to open the door to strangers like that again. That the truck was gone and so was the truck driver.

"Where did they go, Mommy?" asked Veronica.

"They went far away, far away from here...to a place where there are no little children to scare anymore," said Mommy.

"You see," said Daddy, "that man—the one who drove the truck—we've seen him before and he seems very nice, but he's really a bad, bad man and likes to scare little children. Did he try to show you what was in the back of his truck?"

"Yes, Daddy, he did!" shouted Mikey.

"And what did you see there?" asked Mommy.

The children didn't say anything.

"What did you see there?" asked Daddy.

The children didn't know how to answer the question. It was so scary, they didn't know how to answer.

So Mommy said to Daddy, "They don't have to tell us now if they don't want to. Let's give them their presents, Daddy."

"That sounds like a swell idea!" laughed Daddy.

"Oh boy!" Mikey yelped as he opened his present. It was a very big red truck.

"Cool!" he said. "What's in yours, Veronica?"

Veronica opened her present and it was a boy doll that looked just like Dan. "It's the truck driver!" said Veronica. "He was nice—and very handsome!"

"So you see, Mikey and Veronica," said Daddy. "There's really nothing to be afraid of when it comes to big red trucks. There's nothing to be afraid of in this world. The world is a happy place and Mommy and Daddy love you very much, don't we, Mommy?"

"Oh, yes we do, children. We love you more than anything in this world. So there's nothing to be afraid of, and nothing can hurt you."

The brother Mikey and the sister Veronica were very happy after that. And each took their parents' hands as they walked downstairs to have dinner. The truck had gone away, they could see, from the picture window that looked out onto the street. And they felt very safe and secure with Mommy and Daddy—and forgot all about what they saw in the back of the big red truck.

THE END

Well, I didn't know if it would ever be published, but I was amused by my children's book; so having entertained myself for the evening, I decided it was time to retire to the bedroom. I would look over what I had written the next day and perhaps revise it.

I took off my clothes, turned out the lights, and got into bed.

I fell asleep instantly.

I started to dream.

I was on the street where I grew up as a child. The street was deserted. I was the only one there. There were no cars, no other children, and no parents. Everything was very quiet. There were no sounds. I walked alone in the street.

Suddenly I heard a very loud noise, like the noise of an engine, coming my way.

And I saw it again. I had seen it before—only this time it was giant-sized—and it was coming right at me. I couldn't move. I was glued to the spot. It was going to kill me. I was going to die.

But just as it was about to hit me, it stopped. Everything got very quiet again. I walked around toward the back of the truck. I thought to myself, "I'm dreaming—and this is surely a nightmare. Don't walk any further. Don't walk any further. Don't."

But I couldn't stop walking. I walked to the back of the truck and unlatched the door. I looked into the darkness. And I saw...I saw...I saw...AHHHHHHHHHHHHHHHHHHHHHH!!!

I woke up and turned the light on as fast as I could. I put on my robe and went straight to my laptop. I had to write down what I saw. I saw my past, I saw my future, I saw my mind, I saw God. It was the most terrifying sight I ever saw.

PART FOUR: ABSOLUTION

CHAPTER TWENTY-NINE: MICKY

Something very confusing has happened and I'm trying to make sense out of it. I'm a little freaked out.

I wrote that children's book last night and then I had that dream, which I recorded on my laptop. But today I got the strangest letter. It was from the shop where Raven has been.

The first page was an invoice for an enormous bill.

The second page was a letter, saying that they couldn't get Raven to run—and that they'd have to trash him—but that I still owed the money.

And as if that weren't disturbing enough, there was a PS to the letter:

PS: We have cleaned out the contents of your Camaro and found this piece of paper in the glove compartment. We thought you would like to have it, as it looks like it might be a missing chapter from your book. Therefore, we have enclosed it as well. Best of luck with your writing.

I don't know what they're talking about. I haven't written any book except the children's book last night—and how could they know about that? The third page of the letter was something I never saw before:

CHAPTER TWENTY-EIGHT: RAVEN

Apparently, they have done all they can for me. I am on the ground again; I am no longer in pain. Yet I feel entirely numb, as if a blowtorch dulled my mind and senses.

Nobody knows if I can run. They will test me out later today, I imagine. If I run properly, I suppose that Micky will take me back, if he chooses to pay the exorbitant fee. If not, it is the Junkyard for me.

I miss my master. I miss our drives together on the road. I miss the life we knew, pursuing one adventure after another.

Today we will discover our fate; and that will determine the rest of our story. In the meantime, I sit here amongst the other cars who would like to engage me in conversation. But I do not choose to speak with them.

I have nothing more to say.

CHAPTER THIRTY: DAVE

A siren woke me up. It must have been seven in the morning. There were a bunch of police cars turning onto that road up a ways, where I first thought I saw Viagra's car. It was a lot of commotion for that hour, and I needed some coffee and a piss.

Well, I relieved myself by the side of my truck and thought I'd walk up ahead and see what all the fuss was about. I left my rig where it was.

There was a nice-looking police lady at the bottom of the hill, and I suddenly felt a little self-conscious, like I must have looked a little sleepy, you know? A little sand in my eyes? So I tried to act all awake and perky as I got near her.

"Hi," I said. "A little early for all that noise, huh?"

She didn't seem to appreciate my sense of humor and said, "Can I help you with something, sir?"

"Uh, yeah, what's all the fuss about?"

"Someone stole a painting from the artists' colony up there. They're doing an investigation. That your truck?"

"Yeah, that's mine," I said.

"How long have you been there?" she asked.

"Oh, since about two, I guess. I had to pull over for some sleep, you know?"

"Did you see anything suspicious overnight? Any white cars driving by?"

"As a matter of fact," I started to say, but quickly stopped myself for some reason.

"What?" she asked.

"Oh, nothing," I said. "I was just dreaming. Tell me, do you know who stole the painting?"

"We're pretty sure it was a woman named Violet. It was supposed to be her painting, but she wasn't allowed to take it, belonged to the artists' colony. If you ask me, if it *was* her painting, she had every right to take it, but the owner disagrees and is pressing charges. Yeah, Frank," she said into her walky-talky.

"Girl's got another name," the voice said. "Also goes by Viagra. Can you believe that?"

"Viagra! What a laugh!" chuckled the police lady.

I couldn't believe what I heard. So I wasn't dreaming after all. I had to get some coffee so I could think straight. "Excuse me," I said. "Any idea where this woman was going?"

"That's what we're trying to find out. Your guess is as good as mine."

"Well, good luck to you, officer," I said. I still couldn't believe it. "Any idea where I can get a cup of coffee?"

"Yeah, there's a place about a mile down 22 that way. Can't miss it."

"Thanks a lot. Have a good day."

I headed back to my truck to get some coffee and try to figure out what to do next. I had to do something—but I wish I didn't do what I ended up doing.

CHAPTER THIRTY-ONE: VIOLET

I made it. I think. Let me check the address. Yes, it's the right address. I've followed all the directions. But I'm so early. What time is it? 7:15. Gosh, that's early. And I don't even feel tired. I feel adrenalated. Is that a word? Well, that's how I feel: adrenalated!

Artistic Creations: there it is—nice looking store. I found a parking space easily enough; in fact, I had my choice of the whole street. Well, I might as well lock up, stretch my legs and get some coffee, I guess. What are the store hours? Let me see...it opens at 10 A.M. What am I going to do for three hours?

I wish I had a cell phone. I wish I could talk to Max. I wonder what's going on at the Colony. Well, that part of my life is over. This is my new life. Or perhaps I'm between lives—in limbo. Three hours of limbo. I might as well walk around and look at this town, find a place to freshen up and have breakfast.

I enjoyed the ride. Long drives give you plenty of time to think. And I found myself thinking about people, all kinds of people. It seems that everyone has their own particular world, their own way of viewing things. Almost everyone has their own philosophy, often what they were brought up to have. And there's no way to penetrate a person's philosophy; it enfolds them—it locks them in. Ironically, that's what keeps them limited in their thinking, as it protects them from a world that is *un*limited.

Maybe that's why I've had trouble getting along with people. I can't seem to share their point of view. Except with men sometimes. Max came closest, I think, out of all the men I've known. Dave was wonderful—but how well did we really know each other? And Micky... well, Micky—I wonder how we'd get along if we weren't brother and sister. Who knows? Maybe we'd be lovers.

These were the thoughts I had during my drive as I tried to reconcile being an artist with living as a woman in this world. A world filled with such contradictory ideas. How can anyone be sure that his or hers are the correct ones? Yet everyone *seems* so sure, at least by the time they reach a certain age.

I think it's a façade to cover up what they don't really know, what they're not really sure of. By a certain age, you've developed your belief system; and you use it to pretend you understand the world.

I don't want to have a belief system; I'd rather paint others with theirs. And as an artist, illuminate the essence of their thinking, if such a thing is possible. Yes, that's the kind of painting I'm interested in. Take that look of Geramund's, for instance. I want to paint that.

I want to paint a man like Hans and show the dichotomy between integrity and deception. Even if the viewer doesn't understand what I'm trying to say, at least it will look interesting. Let the viewers and critics say what they like. I'll have painted something original, something about the Human Condition.

OK. Enough thinking. I'm hungry. Let me find a place to eat, if anything is open yet. Oh, here comes a little boy. Maybe he'll know.

"Hi there, what's your name?"

"I'm Tommy. Who are you?"

"I'm Violet. What are you doing walking around by yourself so early in the morning?"

"I wanted to see if I could find some flowers for my Mommy. She's sick."

"Oh, what's the matter with her?"

"I don't know. But I'm afraid she's not going to get better. Maybe the flowers will help."

"I'm sure she'll get better, Tommy."

"How come?"

"Because I know that she wouldn't want to leave a sweet, little boy like you. I know she'll get better soon."

"But the doctor said she might not get better. The doctor said we have to be very good to our Mommy because she might not get better."

He's starting to cry, so I kneel down in front of him and stroke his smooth, brown hair. "Now listen to me, Tommy. Do you have any brothers and sisters?"

"Uh-huh," he says, through his tears.

"How many?"

"Just a sister."

"I want you to be very good to your sister and know that whatever happens, everything is going to be OK. You and your sister are going to be fine. Is that a deal?"

"I guess so."

"Have you had breakfast?"

"Yeah."

"Well, I haven't. And I'm hungry. Do you know if there's a place near here where I can get something to eat?"

"There's a place next to where the flowers are—up there. The flowers are in the backyard. That's where I'm going."

"Well, let's walk there together, all right?"

"OK."

I take his hand and we walk down the street of the quiet town together. He has stopped his crying and we don't say anything for a while.

Suddenly a bright red cardinal flies over our heads. "Oh look!" he says.

"It's a cardinal. Isn't it pretty?"

"Where's he flying to?"

"He's going to get breakfast for his family. He's hungry."

We reach the front of a diner and Tommy releases my hand and runs toward the field where the flowers are. "Bye!" he waves, smiling.

"Bye!" I shout as I watch him skip into the field, joyous with his task of flower-picking, oblivious to any sorrow that might be entering his life. He waves back to me once more before running through his field of flowers, as colorful as an artist's palate—designed for transforming our sorrow into something not just beautiful...but without any limiting point of view, something that is right, something that is true.

CHAPTER THIRTY-TWO: MICKY

I found myself on the road. Walking. I had to get out of the house. I had to get away somewhere. I had to get away from myself perhaps, and I needed some fresh air, a chance to breathe.

Something didn't feel right inside of me. Inside of my head. It's difficult to explain. When the shower water came down, for instance, it felt like it was a movie, like it wasn't real, like it wasn't happening to me. And it was a very scary feeling.

I found myself walking in the direction of Raven's garage. I had to see Raven one more time. And I had to ask someone about that piece of paper they found in his glove compartment. This scared me. What could it mean? Was someone playing a joke on me?

It was a long walk to the garage. Should I stick out my thumb, hitch a ride? I hadn't done that in years. Well, I thought, let's try it.

A purple car stopped right away. I'm not kidding. I haven't made up one word that I'm telling you. There was a lady in it. She had purple glasses. The old-fashioned kind. I'll never forget her.

She stopped right after I stuck out my thumb. She had a beautiful smile. She said, "Hello! How far are you going, sir?"

"Uh, not that far...just down to Orange Street...do you know it?"

"Do I know Orange Street! Come on in."

"Thanks."

"Sorry, it's a bit of a mess inside here. I wasn't expecting company. You won't believe what happened to me on Orange Street," she said as we started moving.

"What happened?"

"One day I was driving my car, this purple car, on Orange Street. Sounds pretty funny, I know. The purple and orange. And this huge man...I mean huge, absolutely huge—obese is the word, I guess. This obese man walked right out into the middle of Orange Street and started shouting, 'Where are you going, lady? Where do you think you're going?' Well, I just said to him, 'Sir, you're standing in the middle of the street and I almost hit you. Would you please be more careful?' It's good that he was so enormous, otherwise I might not have seen him, and maybe *would* have hit him. Then he said to me, 'Lady, you shouldn't be driving around this part of town. This is *my* part of town and you shouldn't be driving here.' 'Why not?' I asked him. I had every right to be driving there, of course. Are you following me?"

"Yes, of course," I said. "I'm enjoying your story. What did he say?"

"He just looked at me with a dumbfounded expression...and I'll never forget this, he said, 'Because I'm unhappy in this world and I don't want anyone to see me. I'm ashamed of myself and unhappy in this world. Please go away and don't come back.' I felt sorry for the poor guy, so I said, 'All right. I'll go and I won't come back. But first, let me give you this.' " She paused and looked at me. We were almost there.

"What did you give him?"

"I felt like I should give him something, so I gave him my watch. It had a red cardinal on it—I'll never forget that. I gave him my cardinal watch...and this is the first time I've been back since. Here we are, sir. Orange Street."

"Well, thank you, ma'am," I said. "I appreciate the lift. And I enjoyed your story. Have a good day, now."

"Goodbye, sir. You have a good day, too. And if you run into the fat man, look and see if he's wearing my watch; although it may have been a little dainty for him."

"Oh, if I see him, I will definitely look for the watch. Thanks again."

I got out of the car and the garage was a little ways ahead. I hoped I would run into the fat man, but life is never like that. We never seem to find what we're looking for...at least, not when we want to find it.

The Orange Street Garage was not what I expected it to be. Whoever heard of a car shop playing classical music? Well, they were—the Brahms

Clarinet Quintet—I recognized the piece as I walked in. Everyone was very busy and didn't seem to notice me; so I walked around a bit and tried to find Raven.

All the walls were orange—and they had the hottest mechanics working on the cars there. They were working in varying poses under and over the cars, as if they were about to break out into a sweaty dance, expressing their virile natures—a ballet of car mechanics, which didn't really go with the Brahms Clarinet Quintet.

One of them was heading my way. I got ready and said in my deepest voice, "Excuse me, do you know where my black Camaro is?" I wanted to say goodbye to Raven.

"Yeah, the black Camaro—it's in the back lot."

"Thanks, man."

"Anytime," he smiled, as if it were OK to follow him into the men's room, which is where he seemed to be going. I turned around after passing him; and sure enough, he was going to the men's room; so I decided to make a detour and follow him in there—just for fun.

He was at one of the urinals, so I walked up to the urinal two down from him and pulled it out. I didn't have to go or anything; but this seemed like an amusing diversion in an otherwise strange and upsetting day.

"Did you work on my car by any chance?" I asked him, making sure that he didn't catch me looking down at his dick, which was very hard not to do, for I could see how big it was peripherally, as if he wanted me to see it.

"No, I didn't," he said, "but I heard that they couldn't fix it. Which is weird, cause we're used to fixing all kinds of shit. But they couldn't get the damn thing to run," he said as he shook it, very un-self-conscious and masculine-like. I could have sworn I saw him dart a look down at mine—but he quickly zipped up and headed for the sink.

"Yeah, that's what I heard. I just came here to check it out."

"Well, she's in the back lot—ready to be hauled off."

I wanted to say, "Raven's a *he*," but instead came out with "Thanks a lot, man."

I could have sworn he winked at me in the mirror; but then he walked out. I was never bold enough to get that kind of thing going. Not in a car shop anyway. So I zipped up and walked to the back of the shop to find Raven.

I exited through the back door and spotted him right away. It was going to be tough not to cry. He looked very strange; not really like Raven, but more like a corpse that you see at somebody's wake. I went over to him and put my hand on his hood. I looked around to see if anyone was watching, and then I said, "Goodbye, Raven, if you can hear me. I'm going to miss you, Rave."

I had to turn around real fast and go back inside; otherwise I might have lost it right then and there. I went straight to the office to talk to someone about that piece of paper.

There was an older woman behind the counter. She had car earrings. "Excuse me," I said. "Can I speak to the person who worked on my black Camaro outside?"

"I'm sorry, sir. The young man who worked on your car isn't in today. He had to go to the dentist. Is there anything I can help you with?"

"Yeah, well, I'm wondering who found this piece of paper in my car and if they know anything about it." I showed her the "missing chapter."

"It's the first I've seen it. You probably would need to ask Bill about it. That's his name. He won't be back until next week, though."

"Oh, OK. Thanks."

I walked out of the office and took one more look in Raven's direction as I left the garage and found myself on a dusty, deserted Orange Street.

It was starting to get dark. The wind was blowing gently and I could feel the dust from the street hitting my arms. It felt like I was in a western film. I walked aimlessly on Orange Street, feeling lost, feeling like I had nowhere to go.

I started kicking a white stone. I kicked it, followed it, and kicked it again.

I kept doing this for a while; it seemed to take my mind off the emptiness inside it.

I kicked the stone. I followed it. I kicked it again. I felt very alone. There was no one around. I didn't know what to do. So I kicked the stone and followed it and kicked it again and followed it.

I realized there were tears on my face but no one was there to see them; and I couldn't remember crying but I could feel the tears on my face.

I kicked the stone.

I walked up to where it landed.

It landed next to something. I bent down to see what it was. It was a watch. A watch with a cardinal on it. I picked up the watch and fastened it around my wrist. I didn't see what time it was and I didn't care.

I walked down the street as it got darker. I was feeling lost, scared, alone—but I had found the lady's watch. I wished I knew who she was so I could return it to her. But since I didn't, I'd keep it for myself and always know the time. For you see, I had never worn a watch before.

It felt like it was time for something but I didn't know what.

It was time for my sister to come home. I hoped she would be coming home soon.

CHAPTER THIRTY-THREE: DAVE

After breakfast, I drove back to that place on the road. The police car wasn't there anymore and I wondered if I should go climb that hill, even though I knew that Viagra was gone. Maybe I could find something out and know where to look for her.

I was real disappointed that I missed her. And to think we came so close to seeing each other! Maybe there was someone who could tell me where she went. But if she stole her painting, who would know that? Or want to tell me?

Still, I was up for an adventure. And it was a beautiful morning, so I thought a good walk would do me some good after all that driving.

I secured my truck and was ready for my hike. I walked up to the hill—and boy, did it look steep. It just went way up, like a mini-mountain. Could I really make it on foot if it was so high that it was off the map, like that girl said it was?

Well, I had nothing better to do, so I thought I'd start to climb. And what a climb it was. I mean, I'm an in-shape guy, but still, my endurance was really tested.

I climbed and climbed. And climbed some more. I was starting to get a little winded—I'm a smoker, after all.

Then I saw a car coming down the road my way. It was slowly approaching me, so I kind of waved it down to ask how far the place was.

A dark-haired man with wavy hair was in the car. He was a good-looking guy and seemed real troubled about something.

"Hi," I said. "Do you know how far it is to the artists' colony up there?"

"You've got quite a hike, man. Are you sure you want to do it on foot?"

"Well, I've got no choice. I don't think my truck would make it up this hill. I'm looking for someone, but I don't know if she's there. I think she left this morning."

"Who are you looking for?"

"I know her as Viagra—but I think she goes by the name of Violet, too."

"Oh man, you better get out of here. There's a lot of trouble going on and believe me, you don't want to get involved. Do you know Violet?"

"Yeah, I do. I came all this way to find her."

"Listen," the guy said, "come ride down with me. I'll tell you what happened."

So I got in the car and the guy introduced himself.

"My name's Max," he said as we started down the hill.

"Hi Max, I'm Dave. Glad I ran into you."

"Dave...I think I've heard your name. You're looking for Violet? How did you find out she was here?"

"Long story. Through a friend of hers at work. I drove my truck up here, hoping I'd find her. She left without telling us where she was going. And me and her brother were really worried about her."

"Well, my advice is to stay as far away as possible. Believe me, you don't want to go up there. It's crazy. I needed to get away myself. I almost got arrested, but I talked my way out of it. Were you, uh, involved with Violet?"

"Sort of. In a way. But what happened? How did you almost get arrested?"

"Can I trust you, man? You won't go to the police, will you?"

"Course not. I just want to find her. Do you know where she went?"

"Yeah, I do. See, I helped Violet take her painting last night. They were going to sell it and not give her any of the money. So I helped her get it out of there."

We were getting to the bottom of the hill. "There's my truck—over there," I said.

"OK, I'll drop you off."

"So what happened that you almost got arrested?"

"Well, they assumed that I helped her steal the painting, which I did. I'm not a very good liar, and boy did I lie through my teeth! But a buddy of mine gave me an alibi and got me off the hook, thank God. They were ready to cart me off!"

"Glad things are cool. So where did she go?" We pulled up next to my truck.

"I sent her to my art dealer, about five hours away from here. Let me see if I've got something to write with. I'll give you the directions, if you like. But please, not a word of this to anyone, OK?"

"You've got my word, man."

"It's funny, Dave. I'll tell you, Violet and I got very close. And I've got the feeling you were close with her too. But you know what? I don't feel any kind of competition with you. I feel for that woman; she means a lot to me. So if she's a friend of yours of any kind, I'm sure she'd be glad to see you."

He found a pen and paper and started writing. It looked pretty easy. "Here you go."

"Thanks," I said. "I'm good at directions. I drive for a living."

"Cool. She's at this gallery, Artistic Creations. If you leave now, you should be able to make it by early afternoon."

"Man, I can't tell you how much I appreciate this. I've got to find her. It means a lot to me. Are you going to be all right? You're definitely out of trouble?"

"I think so. I just need to chill, take a drive. Good luck," he said, as he reached out to shake my hand. "When you see Violet, tell her that Max sends his regards."

"Oh, I will. Violet—sounds funny to me. But I guess Viagra sounds even funnier to you."

"We're used to it," he laughed. "Most of the people up there change their names. I was one of the few who kept mine. You see, I refuse to change. Ha, ha. I'm just the same guy I always was. Take care, Dave. Make sure that Violet's OK, will you?"

"You bet. Thanks again."

I got out of his car and jumped up on my truck. I had another good drive ahead of me—and I was as high as a red bird in the sky. My ears were red with excitement, that is. I started her up and got back on 22, beginning my journey to find my love. I knew I was getting closer. After all, this was my lucky day.

I was so happy. God, was I happy. Happy, free, another drive ahead of me.

I started singing:

Happy, free

Another drive ahead of me

It was my lucky day. And I really believed it at the time.

CHAPTER THIRTY-FOUR: VIOLET

When I heard much later how Dave tried to find me, I was surprised and moved. When we realize the true circumstances that lead us to our current places in life, it can be an overwhelming discovery. For as touched as I was to learn of Dave's love for me, it nevertheless came as quite a shock after the dramatic events that occurred.

As I look back on it now, I see that Dave was an important catalyst in my life; and in many ways, I have him to thank—for his love, yes, but mostly for his sacrifice.

It may seem that Max was the logical choice for me; but I will always remember Dave as the man responsible for the life I know.

After a leisurely breakfast, I walked back to the gallery, and it was already open by the time I arrived. I walked in and was surrounded by an impressive array of paintings, sculptures, and pottery. It felt good to know that my work might be a part of this place, a place that had the sweet scent of art in its midst.

An attractive man with a dark moustache and goatee greeted me with a friendly smile. "Hello," he said, "we're not officially open yet. But feel free to browse around, if you like."

"Thank you," I said. "My name is Violet. Did you get a call from Max yet, by any chance?"

"Violet! Hello! My name is Larry. Larry Kipper. Good to meet you."

"Good to meet you, too, Larry. This is a beautiful shop."

"Thanks. Yes—Max called me this morning and told me all about you. That's why I'm opening a little early. I assumed you'd be arriving in the wee hours. How was your drive?"

"Invigorating. I love long drives."

"Have you had breakfast?"

"Yes, I just did—at the diner down the road."

"Oh, I wish I had known. I would have brought something for you. Is your painting outside? I can't wait to see it. Max said it's amazing—and if Max says it's amazing, that's good enough for me. I'm sure you're a very talented painter."

"Well, it's the first painting I've done in years. But I'm planning to start my work again, and would love to be a part of this here, if you'd like to represent it."

"Let's go get it and bring it in, have a look. I'm excited!"

His exuberance told me that he was gay. Heterosexual men never get quite so enthusiastic about anything at that hour of the morning. And I was glad that I wouldn't have to deal with any kind of romantic attraction. I had had enough of that for a while.

We walked out to my car and Larry helped me untie my painting and carry it inside to the back of the shop. He unwrapped it carefully, undoing all of Max's knots, and when he finally stepped back and gave it a look, he let out a big gasp.

"This is totally awesome!" he said. "Wow! How long did it take you to do this?"

"A couple of weeks. You like it?"

"I love it. I would be proud to have it in my store. I can't believe it's the first thing you've done in years. You have a natural talent—Max was right. I'd be glad to show your work here."

"Oh, Larry. I don't know what to say. Thank you. I suppose this is what most artists dream of. I'm very grateful."

"It's my pleasure, Violet. Do you have plans of painting more soon? I could put them in the window. We have people from all over the country coming here. And there's a very good chance that you'll be reviewed in prestigious art journals—not to mention the living you'll be able to make from your work. Forgive me, I'm just flabbergasted. I don't make discoveries like this every day."

"I don't hear praise like this every day either. Thank you so much. It's a little overwhelming, to tell you the truth. Yes...I intend to paint more very soon; in fact, I've got a few ideas already. But I just left the artists' colony where Max is, and I have to think about getting resettled at home and setting up my studio there."

"Oh, of course, of course. Take your time. But just know that you've got a home here when you want it. Based on what I see...whoa, it really is intense! You've got quite a career cut out for you, you know that? How far away do you live?"

"I think about three hours, if I've figured it right. You're somewhere between the Colony and my house. I could easily bring my work up here when it's finished."

"Nonsense...we'll ship it for you."

"Oh, that's very kind of you—but I enjoy the driving, especially with a completed painting strapped to my roof! It's a very fulfilling feeling!"

"I'll bet it is!" he laughed.

We spent a few minutes grinning at each other, looking at the painting, and then looking back at each other. I felt like I had a new friend.

"Have you taken many classes?" he asked.

"Only a few, when I was a little girl."

"Uncanny. It shows you what too much education can do. I've seen many artists who get their degrees at universities—and the academia just squelches their natural talent. It's really not something you can study too much. May I ask you, who is that man?"

"It's my father."

"Ah. Then that's you as a little girl, I suppose. Forgive me, I don't mean to pry."

"No, it's all right. I've got no secrets. I was an abused child. But painting this helped to release that for me. I feel like a new woman."

"Congratulations. Your entire past has gone onto that canvas. Better than twenty years of therapy, huh?"

"Definitely!" I chuckled. And we had a good laugh together. I knew we were going to be great friends.

I was back on the road again, heading home. Home. I was glad to be returning because I now had a reason to live: I would set up a studio in my house and become a full-time artist. Come hell or high water, I would have a fulfilling life.

Oh, I thought, I should call Micky. Let him know I was on my way.

I pulled over to the first service area I saw, found a phone and dialed his number. Naturally, I got his machine:

"Hello, this is Micky. I've gone for a walk and I don't know when I'll be back. Please leave a message, and if I ever come back, perhaps I will speak to you soon."

"Hi Micky! Guess who? It's Viagra, but I don't use that name anymore; I go by Violet now—long story. I'm on my way home and I've got a lot to tell you. Can't wait to see you, hope you're OK. I should be there in a few hours, so call me—if you ever come back! Bye!"

His voice sounded strange, as if he were hiding an inner desperation somehow; but perhaps it was my imagination. I hoped he was all right.

I looked forward to seeing him. I missed my brother. I couldn't wait to tell him about my new life—my life as an artist, my life as a new woman.

I got back in my car and turned on the radio. They were playing Dvořák's *New World Symphony*. Perfect. What a perfect day. What a lucky day. It was truly my lucky day.

I had no idea, of course, what awaited me at home; no idea of the events that were about to unfold; no idea of the truths that were about to cement themselves into reality—the reality that was to become, and still is, the life I was meant to have.

CHAPTER THIRTY-FIVE: DAVE

You know, it's really weird, but I feel like there are chunks of time in my life that I can't account for, that I don't remember. I don't mean over ten years ago, which I told you about, but more recent-like. Like I'll be waking up one morning on the highway, and I can't seem to remember where I was for the last few days.

This has happened to me for a while. It doesn't interfere with my work or my driving or anything. And my memory seems normal in other ways—most ways, like remembering people's names and stuff. But sometimes I just can't tell you what I did for the last few days, no matter how hard I try to remember.

Weird. But I don't worry about it too much. I still feel happy, especially when I'm driving, like I am right now, driving to find Viagra—and I'm almost there! I've got the directions memorized. See? My memory's OK. I'm on Route 107 right now. I've just got one more turn-off and then I'm there. Oh boy! I can't wait! And what a surprise it'll be for Viagra when I get there! I can't wait to see the look on her face!

But, you know, sometimes I try to figure out the things I've done during the times I can't remember. I must have done something—did I blot it all out? I mean, I'm an adult. I've always thought of myself as a pretty normal guy. Hell, I'm good-looking, friendly—I like girls, and a guy every now and then. What's wrong with that?

But I've been thinking that when I find Viagra, I never want to let her get away from me again. When I find her, maybe it's time to settle down with her. Maybe get married, have kids, the way most people do. It's a good way to live, I guess. Having a family. Keeps you safe. Keeps you feeling like you belong to the world, like you're part of the human race, you know? Maybe that's what I should have now. I'm not getting any younger, and maybe it's time I joined the normal world.

Hell, I'd never give up my driving. But if I could come home to a woman like Viagra and maybe a kid too, wouldn't that be a good way to live? It's about time I started thinking about this kind of stuff, like most people do. Hey—that's what makes the world go round, isn't it? Having a family, raising kids, being a part of the world?

Well, first let me find her and then we can make our plans. I know we've got something special together—and I also know she feels the same way. Of course, I'm going to have to apologize for not calling her sooner. And I'm going to have to deal with what Micky told me. I'm going to have to ask her about it, find out more.

But hell, if she's crazy, what do I care? I know that I love her now, crazy or not. She's just a great woman—the best I've ever known. I would do anything for her. I'd give my life for her, I really would.

Well, looks like we're coming to the last turn-off. Here it is, Exit 2, Red Berry Road. I just have to go about a mile on Red Berry Road and then I think I'm there. I love following directions. They're like playing a game, a treasure game—and when you figure out how to get there, you can find the treasure. I especially like it when the directions are confusing—it's fun to figure them out. But these were easy. OK, I'm turning right onto Red Berry Road...nice scenery around here, lots of rolling fields and hills and farms. I've never been around here before.

OK, I'm looking for the numbers. Looks like it'll be on the right side of the road, but I've still got a ways to go.

How about some music? Let's see what I can get. Oh, I know this music. Don't know what it's called, though. Some kind of symphony, I guess. Very exciting and dramatic. I bet you'd recognize it. Puts me in the right kind of mood to see Viagra again.

Makes me want to drive fast. Sometimes I have trouble controlling my speed if the music really gets to me. I've just got to fly with the music, you know? I've just got to breeze down the road, the Red Berry Road—I like that!

I'm going faster—I love my speed—I love my power. I'm a king. I'm a god of the road. A flying king, a flying god—soaring higher with the music....

I am Dave, the Eternal One

I am free, like the Golden Sun

I soar, I fly, I speed, I go

Where was I yesterday? I don't know!

Ha-hah! The power of the music makes me go faster, faster to my love, faster to the clouds, the heights of time....

I am the heights of time

I am a driver divine

There's my landmark...a diner on the left...I'm almost there...faster, faster, I'm almost there!

Oh Christ, a little kid with a bunch of flowers is running toward me—FUCK—he's going to run in front of me—FUCK—I can't stop—I can't stop—I'm going to hit him—

OH NO! I'M GOING TO HIT HIM! OH MY GOD!!!

Oh my God. I've hit the little kid. Oh my God. Oh my God.

I tried to slam on the brakes but I've hit the little kid. Oh no...I've killed him...I've killed the little kid....

Everything's going black. I'm passing out. I don't know where I am. I'm not here. I'm not anywhere.

I don't remember. I don't remember. It's all gone dark. It's all gone away.

I'm not here anymore.

I heard a child's screaming voice

Somewhere the other day

But don't remember where it was

Or why it was that way

I've gone somewhere on a long, long trip

Somewhere far away

But don't remember where I've gone

Or if I plan to stay....

147

CHAPTER THIRTY-SIX: MICKY

I don't remember how I got home. I remember walking up to the front door, opening it, and seeing my living room all dark with just a red light blinking, like a night ambulance flashing on the side of the road. The light made a red reflection on the wall—on and off, on and off—and I had to wonder if I was really in my house, or instead, perhaps, some prison cell with a red girlie neon sign outside.

But I knew it was just my phone machine and that I had a message. Who could be calling me? Dave? I turned on the lights and pressed the button on the machine. It was Viagra!

"Hi Micky! It's Viagra! I'm on my way home and I should be there very soon. Call me when you get this. I can't wait to see you and tell you everything. I love you. Bye."

Ah, my sister was finally coming home. I was very glad. And although I had just gotten back myself, I couldn't wait to get out of the house again; the walls seemed to be closing in on me. I picked up the phone and called my sister.

"Hello?" she said.

"Viagra. Hi, it's Micky."

"Micky! It's so good to hear your voice! How are you?"

"I don't know; not so good. Raven died and I was just at the garage saying goodbye to him."

"Oh, I'm sorry to hear that. How are you getting around?"

"Walking, mostly, and a little hitchhiking. V, can I ask you something?"

"Sure."

"What are you doing tonight?"

"Tonight?"

"Yeah, I feel weird, like I shouldn't be alone." I was trying to hold back my tears. "Can I sleep over?"

"Uh...sure, I guess. I'm just getting resettled here. I'm a little crazed; but I guess that would be OK. Are you all right, Micky?"

"I don't know, honey. I'm...a little...." I started to cry.

"Micky, honey? Do you want me to come and get you?"

"No, that's OK. I'll call for a taxi. It'll be really good to see you.... Viagra?"

"Yes?"

"Oh, nothing, I forgot what I was going to say."

"You heard in my message that I changed my name, right?"

"No. Are you sure you told me?"

"Yeah, pretty sure; I could have sworn I told you. Anyway, I go by Violet now—so if it's possible, can you call me that?"

"I'll try, but it might not be easy. How about V? Will that be OK?"

"Sure, that's fine. Listen, Micky, I'm worried about you. You don't sound so good."

"I'm not so good, I don't think. That's why I want to come stay with you. I'm feeling like...I don't know, V. I miss our childhood. I miss our old house and everything. I've been having some weird dreams. But it'll be good to see you. I've missed you."

"Aw, I've missed you too, honey. I've got a lot to tell you. So what time shall I expect you? I'll make a bed for you in the living room."

"How about a half hour? I found a watch today. It's got a red cardinal on it. It's now 9:06. So about 9:36?"

"That sounds good...."

"V?"

"Yes?"

"Sorry, you sounded distant."

"Oh, I was just thinking about someone. The cardinal reminded me. A cute little boy I met today. I hope he's going to be all right."

"Where did you meet him?"

"Long story. I'll tell you later. Let me get things ready for you. I'll see you soon, OK?"

"OK, Violet. Violet...sounds funny. I'll have to get used to it."

"Oh, you will, I'm sure. I'm not changing it back!"

"OK, V, see you soon."

We both kissed the receiver like we used to do and I tried to figure out if I should call a taxi or walk. But as I said, the walls were closing in on me—and I didn't feel like looking up the number and waiting...so I turned off the lights and left my house again.

The cardinal told me it was 9:09. Strange to always know the time. Time to do this. Time to do that. Time to clean up. Time to go. Time to get there. Time for...a great adventure. A great achievement. A great destiny.

It was time for...the Great Beyond.

I started walking toward my sister's. Funny, I had never walked there before. The half-moon was up in the sky next to what looked like a planet. I think it was Saturn. You could tell it was a planet because it wasn't twinkling. That's how you could tell. Or so they said.

I walked toward my sister's with the moon and Saturn as my guides. I was lost and lonely and looked forward to the comfort of my sister's arms. Her arms, her voice, her smile, her lips...which I knew would make everything all right again. Just like it used to be. Just like the old days, when it was just me and Viagra and the deep love we had for each other...and would soon be having again once more.

CHAPTER THIRTY-SEVEN: VIOLET

I'll never forget the look on my brother's face when I saw him at my door that night. It was the look of someone who had seen too much of life, someone who had experienced all of its degradation and hopelessness. His smile seemed to have lost all of its childhood joy, as if he knew what was in store for him—what was in store for both of us.

When you realize that someone you love is about to begin their descent into madness, you feel that you want to do everything you can to preserve their little comforts, to be as loving as possible; for the look that I saw in his eyes that night was just the beginning. And yet it foretold all of the events that were about to occur. It was the look of someone who could see beyond time, as if he had seen God, perhaps, and didn't care for what he saw.

"Oh, Micky, it's so good to see you," I said as I opened the door.

"Viagra! Sorry...Violet."

"That's OK, don't worry about it."

"I'll try my best. Give me a hug."

We embraced with all the warmth of the olds days; it felt so good to be with my brother again. For there was a long stretch of time when the two of us were all we had in the world. His musky scent and his furry hair made me feel loved and needed; yet it reminded me of a time when I was much weaker. And now it seemed like I would have to be the strong one.

"Where have you been all this time?" he asked. "We were worried about you."

"I was staying at an artists' colony. I've become an artist again. But this time, for real! Who's 'we?' "

"Uh...me and Dave."

"Dave? You know Dave?"

"Yeah, I do. I helped him to go find you. Did you see him?"

"No, I never did. Wait a minute...maybe that *was* his truck last night. Sorry, honey, so much has happened, it's all a little confusing to me. You sent Dave to go and find me?"

"Yeah, I did."

"Well, how did you know where I was?"

"I called Frieda at your job and she gave me a rough idea, but she wasn't sure. Did you see Dave's truck?"

"I thought I saw one that looked just like it as I was leaving last night. I can't believe it was just last night. I haven't slept at all."

"I've hardly slept either. It's been a very intense time."

"So how do you know Dave? How did you get in touch with him?"

He looked at me blankly, like he didn't know what to say.

"Micky?" I asked.

"Yes," he said.

"How do you know Dave?"

He paused again and then he looked at his watch. "See my new watch?" he asked. "It's time."

"Time?"

"Yes, time."

"Time for what?"

"I don't know. Time for something. Time for bed?"

"That's not a bad idea. I could use some sleep. I've made up the couch here all nice for you. I hope it'll be comfortable."

We walked over to the opened couch and sat down on it together. He took my hand and said, "Oh, V...life is hard sometimes, you know?"

"I do know, honey, I really do. But you can't give in to the hardness; you've got to overcome it, no matter what happens. Remember when Mommy and Daddy died? I was eight and you were ten. It was a month after my England daddy disappeared. And we were all alone. Aunt Ella was hardly ever there. Do you remember what you told me?"

"No...what did I tell you?"

"You told me to always be strong and brave and that nothing could

152

hurt me. That the world was a happy place and that nothing could hurt me."

"I don't remember telling you that."

"Well, I remember. It's what kept me going for a long time. And you know what?"

"No...what?"

"It took me years to believe that it might be true. I'm only just now starting to think there might be some truth in what you said."

There was a long silence between us.

Then suddenly he said, "V...I'm scared."

"Scared of what?" I asked.

"Just scared." And he started to cry. He lay his head down on my lap and cried.

I petted his curly hair and whispered, "It's OK, just let it out, let it all out...."

"Aw, V..." he said, choking up, "being different from everyone else is not an easy way to be."

"I know, I know."

After a little while he stopped crying and said, "Thank you, honey. You are so good, you are so beautiful. You're the best sister." And he sat up and gave me a warm kiss on my neck.

"I think we're both a little exhausted. Why don't we talk tomorrow and catch up on everything, huh? After we've both had a good night's sleep?"

"That sounds good," he said. "Thanks for everything."

"Anytime, Micky. That's what sisters are for. I've put out a towel for you in the bathroom, and there's a beer in the fridge if you want it. Tomorrow we'll go and get some food for a nice dinner, if you like."

"Oh, that'd be swell. We can get some nice wine, too. I'll look forward to that."

"Goodnight, sweetie. I'll see you tomorrow. Get some sleep, now."

"You too, V. Goodnight."

And I left him there in the living room as I got ready to sleep in my own bed for the first time in a while. I was worried about Micky but didn't yet realize the seriousness of the situation.

For my brother and I were traveling in opposite directions; and the next few days would be the last time we would share the same level, the same plane of existence. For I was on a skyrocket to the stars, while he seemed to be spiraling downward into a pit of darkness. And there was nothing I could do except to offer my love...and wait for Dave to return...to give us his ultimate gift.

CHAPTER THIRTY-EIGHT: MICKY

It was very late at night and my sister appeared in the doorway, wearing a light blue nightgown. She seemed almost like a spirit, a light blue phantasm of my imagination. Her flowing gown blew in the breeze; and she was, as always, a vision of love and beauty.

She walked slowly toward my bed and pulled back the covers. I lay there naked, half-asleep and said, "Hi...I'm glad you're here. Come spend the night with me."

She removed her gown and got into bed beside me, pulling the covers over us.

"I couldn't sleep," she said. "And I was worried about you. I wanted to make sure you were all right."

"I'm fine with you here next to me, V. I'm always fine when you're here."

I reached over and started kissing her lips. She returned my kiss, moaning gently, saying, "Oh, Micky...it's so good to be with you again."

I decided not to answer, but to let actions speak louder than words. I kissed her deeply, feeling myself aroused. We kissed like distant lovers of the past, while the breeze blew over us and very faint music entered the window, serenading our lovemaking: music from the highway, the late night cars and trucks creating a quiet symphony of their own.

I couldn't help myself and said, "Viagra...I love you...I've always loved you," as I got on top of her, my erection feeling so manly and strong against her soft pubic hair.

We kissed and rolled over and caressed each other. It was beautiful— as beautiful as I remembered it from long ago.

She said, "Micky...oh, Micky...."

And I said, "V...my very own, my blood, my life...."

And I entered her with all my passion and strength; I entered my sister—and we were one with the night, one with nature. It was a holy act. The two of us were entranced in our love as we rose to a higher plane, a place outside of our bodies, a place that we remembered from some distant time, some distant land. We were no longer in our bodies; we had become transcendent beings, one with the stars.

I started to come and she was right with me. We screamed together, we screamed with ecstasy. We kissed each other deeply and became gods, the two of us, coming together with the breeze and the music and the stars and the night. It surpassed anything I had ever experienced. For I was with my beloved and we were one with the night.

We drifted into sleep as I stayed inside her, not wanting to lose what we had found again, our very special love long forgotten and cast aside. We slept together like that for as long as I can remember...until the morning light awakened me, and I realized she had returned to her own bed to dream separate dreams once more.

But I looked forward to spending the day with her...and the ensuing nights that would surely follow.

CHAPTER THIRTY-NINE: VIOLET

You may wonder how two children who lost their parents could live alone in a house all by themselves. As an adult, I've marveled at this myself; but have drawn the conclusion that it was our love for each other that kept us alive. After the initial trauma of our parents' death, which of course hit us very hard, Micky and I slowly became happy living together. He seemed so grown up to me then.

Aunt Ella, our mother's sister, was supposed to be taking care of us. Neither of us liked her very much, though; she wore these outrageous hats, which Micky and I found pretentious. But she brought us our food every day; and this was when Micky discovered his natural talent for cooking. I used to call him Chef Mické. We had gourmet meals with classical music nearly every night, just like we did with our parents. And we always made sure that the candles were lit; we were trying to recreate the ambiance of our family meals.

We were very lucky with the authorities. It seemed like every time they checked up on us, Aunt Ella was there, bringing her daily ration of food; and after a while, they stopped bothering us. We just wanted to be left alone. And of course, I didn't miss my real father at all. It wasn't until months later that his body was found; but the details of his death and suicide were kept from us for years.

My mother had had a brief affair with my English father when she was staying in London, finishing her art degree, while Micky's father took care of him here in the States. Apparently, they had a somewhat open marriage; and there didn't seem to be any jealousy on either of their parts regarding their occasional flings. But from what I heard, it wasn't entirely easy for Seymour to accept Sylvia's pregnancy with me; yet he gradually came to terms with it and raised me as his own daughter.

The trouble started when Garrick came to visit. He was a sick, miserable man—definitely an alcoholic—and this was when I experienced his abuse, unbeknownst to the rest of the family. I didn't know how to tell anyone about it; and he threatened actual death if I ever mentioned it.

After all of them had left us, Micky and I spent our days going to school, our evenings studying and eating our gourmet dinners, and our nights in the same bed, falling asleep in each other's arms. In many ways, it was a beautiful existence; yet neither of us realized the pain that was buried until much later. It was all we could do at the time to survive. And survive we did—with each other.

It was a pleasure to have Micky staying with me again, as he had done several times since our childhood; and it was comforting to know how much we still cared for each other. I was happy to see him asleep in the sofa bed as I tiptoed to the kitchen to make coffee. As much as I had been through in the last few weeks, it was wonderful to have my brother around—and to know that he needed me.

"Good morning, V," I heard him call from the living room.

"Hi honey, did you sleep all right?"

"Best sleep I've had in a long time."

He walked into the kitchen with his sheet wrapped around him, looking like a sleepy Greek hero, ready for his morning walk to the Parthenon.

"Look at you!" I laughed, noticing his hair all crushed on one side.

"What?"

"Oh, nothing, you look funny! Are you feeling better?"

"Yeah, I think so. It was really nice sleeping over."

"Well, you can stay as long as you like. It's great to have you, honey. What would you like for breakfast? I don't have much here yet. Your choices are toast and coffee or toast and tea."

"I'll take coffee."

"Great. That's what I'm making. Butter or marmalade?"

"Both."

"You've got it."

"Very English, you know, butter and marmalade."

"I know. So what would you like for dinner?"

"Dinner? I don't know yet...it's so early...what would you like?"

"Hmmm...how about..."

"Wait a minute. Don't tell me," he said, raising his hand. "Why are you thinking about having pork tonight when you know you'd rather have fish?"

"Micky! What did you just say?"

"You heard me correctly, Viagra."

"You just read my mind again!"

"That's good. It shows I haven't lost my touch. And I'd rather have fish myself. I'm actually in the mood for white wine which doesn't go as well with pork."

"Well cool, after breakfast we'll go to the market and stock up. Feel like making a fancy dinner?"

"You know I do. Got any OJ? My mouth is parched."

"No, we'll have to get some. I'm out of everything. Remember, I haven't been here."

We gazed at each other with wide eyes, as if our entire childhood came back to us right then and there, and we gave each other a big hug. I hoped he had slept off whatever was ailing him, that it wasn't as serious as I had feared.

For he seemed so happy that morning. And it was one of the last times I remember seeing my brother happy, as if he'd had a special dream overnight and was still living it. The light shone through the kitchen window, casting bright auras around each of us, while a Mendelssohn string symphony played on the little radio by the stove.

I poured our coffee and we toasted our time together. "Here's to being with you again," he said, clicking his mug against mine.

It was the last day the two of us would share this kind of happiness; and it's a memory that I cherish: the morning light shining on my brother in his tunic, smiling at me like a Greek hero with smushed hair.

CHAPTER FORTY: MICKY

Ah, it was nighttime again, the secret dark time when lovers' souls unite, when their inmost hearts become one with their dreams, and they are able to fly away from the world, retreat to a place in their imaginations that only they share, that no one else can experience.

Our day together was fun enough—driving, shopping, cooking, reminiscing—and wining and dining, just like the old days. But after a glorious evening with my sister, I looked forward to an even more glorious night; and I could tell by the glint in her eyes over dinner, the way the candles cast their flames into her eyes, the way the music lilted in our ears, that the night would surpass all of our previous days.

I waited in my bed until I felt the time was right. I didn't want to look at the cardinal; I wanted to *feel* the time was right; I had to know it was the perfect time. For tonight I wouldn't wait for Viagra—I was going to *her* room this time; I was going to *her* bed. And everything would be balanced and perfect in the world once again; a world that was full of imperfection, soon to be perfected by our love.

Did I hear a chime in the distance? It was time. I rose from my bed, naked, and felt as if I floated, almost, toward my sister's bedroom. I floated through the dark; I could see in the dark; I could feel my way toward the scent of my sister, like an animal sensing the direction of his prey, though my prey was my reward, my love, my happiness forever.

I entered her bedroom and she was expecting me, I could tell. The covers were pulled back on the side of the bed to make room for me; and as I entered she raised her arm in midair and beckoned for me to approach her. She waved me closer, coaxing me on, until I lay in her bed, fresh with the smell of her perfume, her nighttime fragrance of lavender and rose, or whatever it was, that made her who she was, the special love woman she was.

I joined her in her bed; I joined her in her arms; and we held each other, glad to be together again, glad that our childhood was now our adulthood, that we had now come full circle—and were ready for our late night bliss together.

We held each other; and there didn't seem to be any need to make love that night. Perhaps it was the wine, but we just drifted off, feeling that sense of rapture when you fall asleep in the arms of the person you love—and know that you are safe from the world, that nothing can hurt you, that no one can be cruel....

I was standing on the street in front of my old school. Everyone I knew was there: my teachers, my classmates, Viagra, my parents; it must have been visiting day—it must have been a fire drill—why else would we be outside in front of the school? We were told to line up against the brick wall. Something was scary about this. I didn't know what but something felt very scary.

I heard a loud noise in the distance. We all heard it—we all turned our heads—and we saw this tremendous red truck coming straight at us from down the road. It was approaching faster and faster, heading straight toward all of us. It was going to hit us and we all started screaming. Even the parents were screaming—even the teachers were screaming.

And then the truck plowed into all of us together and killed us. I could feel the truck push up against my stomach. But it happened so fast that it didn't even hurt. I was dead and it didn't even hurt. In a way, it felt good, because I was flying over the school and waving goodbye to everyone. I flew higher and higher, but I heard the voice of my sister down below. I heard Viagra's screaming voice; I heard the voices of the other children, too. They didn't realize that it was nice to be dead and to fly up to heaven, to freedom. They were all stuck down on earth and didn't know how to fly.

But when I heard Viagra screaming, I realized I had to fly down to get her. So I flew down and grabbed her hand and said, "Come on, fly with me...."

But she didn't stop screaming...and then I woke up and Viagra really *was* screaming. I said, "Hey, hey, honey, what's the matter?"

And she said, "Oh...Micky, I was having that dream again—only this time we were at school...and the red truck came to kill us...the red truck came to take us away...."

"Shhh," I said, glad that I could comfort *her* this time, "I was having the same dream...at school. Were Mommy and Daddy there?"

"Yes, they were there. They were in the dream. But we all died...and the last thing I remember was you flying down to take me away with you."

"That's the last thing I remember, too. We were having the same dream at the same time. Do you know what that means?"

"No, what does it mean?"

"I don't know. That we're both crazy?"

"Oh, Micky," she laughed. "Don't tease me. You're not even really here. I'm just dreaming that you are."

"No, I'm here, honey, I'm here."

"It sure seems like you're here. How did you feel when you saw Mommy and Daddy again?"

"I don't remember much of Daddy, but seeing Mommy was...I don't know...she looked real pretty...I don't remember too well. I hardly remember her at all; I've blocked it all out."

"Well, I remember Daddy being so warm and cuddly and friendly to me. I saw him in the dream and he winked at me...like it was all a big joke, like life was a big joke, and even the red truck coming was a big joke—and that we shouldn't take it too seriously. Something like that. But it's like it really happened. Something like that really happened when he was alive, only I don't remember it exactly."

"I know what you mean. I can hardly remember Sylvia; but when I saw her in the beginning of the dream, there was something so warm, so distantly warm and loving about her. Like a love I don't remember, like a part of the world that used to be friendly and kind, but that doesn't exist anymore, you know?"

"I know exactly what you mean...."

"I'm so glad...I'm so glad...."

Our conversation faded away after that. We cuddled together in Viagra's bed and it felt so good that we just drifted away...we drifted back into dreamland...back into the imagined place behind our minds, where the world disguises its true meaning, and presents us with images from another realm, a realm that is different from the world we know.

I was spinning in a counter-clockwise direction; I was spinning beyond time. I was traveling across the Atlantic Ocean. I passed over London—I could see Big Ben, like in *Peter Pan*—and I thought, "Should I go there?" But somehow it didn't feel quite right, so I ventured further and I was suddenly over the Eiffel Tower. I thought, "Let's go to Paris—let's go to Paris again." So I parachuted down to Paris and landed on the *Champs Elysées*. How wonderful it was to be in Paris again. I passed by McDonald's and thought, "Oh, there's the *Arc de Triomphe*! But where's Viagra?" I didn't see her anywhere.

Then all of a sudden, a big red truck appeared in the distance. I could see it all the way down at *Place de la Concorde*, heading my way.

It was happening in slow motion—and I was hyper aware of everything. The truck was coming closer and closer. And when the truck got extremely close, still in slow motion, I could see the driver for the first time.

I couldn't believe who the driver was. The truck was about to hit me—and the driver was Dave. Dave, my buddy. Dave, my other love. And he was going to kill me.

I woke up in my own bed in the living room. I was alone again. Without Viagra, without Dave, and without any idea of what was happening, except the burning sensation that it was time for something momentous: it was time to discover myself. And from that moment on, it was my mission to uncover my soul—to ascertain who I was—to make peace with my life, with the world, with my inner mind.

For there was one thing I was sure of: Dave was driving in our direction. He was coming toward us...and he was coming very soon.

CHAPTER FORTY-ONE: DAVE

My beeper woke me up. I could feel it vibrating in my pocket. Where was I? I wasn't sure—on the side of some road. I took the beeper out of my pocket and saw my boss's telephone number. I had to find a phone. He probably had a delivery for me.

I had a bad headache. Did I go out drinking the night before? I couldn't remember. I couldn't remember what I was doing. I decided to walk off my hangover, or whatever it was, so I locked up my truck and took a little hike.

There were a lot of yellow flowers on the shoulder of the road—and I didn't recognize where I was at all. What was happening to my memory? Was I becoming senile at my age?

I came to a parking area and there was a public telephone there. So I called my boss and he answered the phone.

"Delivery," he said.

"Hi, Shel, it's Dave."

"Dave! Where have you been, man? I've been trying to get a hold of you. I've got a big drop-off for you. Are you loaded up?"

"Far as I know."

"Good. This is a big one. Don't mess it up. You got a pencil?"

"Yeah, just a sec." I got out my pen and pad.

"It's off of Route 99—Elysian Boulevard. You know it. Just off 99. Number 123 Elysian Boulevard. Let them take everything—it's a big order. You got it?"

"Yeah, 123 Elysian Boulevard."

"Good. Call me when you're done. You'll need to load up again."

"OK, Shel. I'll call you."

"Cool. Later."

Good. I was going to be near Micky and Viagra's. It would be great to see them. Wait a minute—I was trying to find Viagra. Where was she? Did she get home yet? I just couldn't remember. Fuck. What was happening to me?

I walked back to my truck and looked forward to seeing my two favorite people. Hell, I couldn't think of anyone I cared for as much as Micky and Viagra. They were very special to me. As soon as I figured out where I was, I'd be off in their direction. Funny how your life takes you in the right direction.

I was excited about seeing them. My best buddy and my favorite girl. I'd be seeing them real soon—and everything in my life would make sense again.

CHAPTER FORTY-TWO: VIOLET

The bacon sizzling on the kitchen stove reminded me of the coffee shop where my mother used to take me as a little girl. The smell of bacon cooking has always reminded me of that—and what it was like to have a mother. I don't know where Micky was on these occasions; perhaps he was in school. It was just my mother and I, and it was a very special feeling.

"What do you want to be when you grow up, Viagra?" I remember her asking me.

"I don't know, Mommy. Maybe a famous artist."

"Well, that's a lot of hard work, honey. And it's a lonely life. I know because I've studied the lives of many artists. It may seem glamorous to us now, but it's a very hard life."

"That's OK, Mommy, if I can paint a beautiful painting, that's all that matters to me."

And I still feel the same way. I only wish I stuck with my painting when I was younger, that it didn't take so long to remember how much it meant to me. I always associated the smell of bacon with that little scene, perhaps the most vivid I have of my mother.

I wondered how Micky was doing. He seemed pretty good the evening before; and I hoped that our visit together was curing him of his ills. I was soon to discover, though, that this was far from the truth.

He entered the kitchen wearing a suit and tie—not at all like Micky—and said, "Good morning, V, that bacon smells good."

"Hi honey, look at you—did you sleep well?"

"Not really; but you know that."

"I do? How could I know?"

"You just do...you know...it's time."

"Time for what?" There was something vaguely disconcerting whenever he said that.

"Time for breakfast. And time for serious work."

"What kind of work?" I asked.

"Work on the self, work on the psyche; what other kind of work is there?"

"Well, there's my artwork, for one thing—and today I have to get some supplies. Do you want to come with me?"

"No, I think I'll stay home and work on myself. You can go to your job...and I'll watch all the people going to work. That'll be fun. They all go to work. Everyone does that. You know?"

"Well, most people do," I said, perplexed by what he was saying.

"That's *all* most people do, even you, Violet. See? I got it right."

"I'm very impressed," I said, serving us breakfast. I sat down at the table. "Where did you get those clothes?"

"From the hall closet. I left them there for an emergency, remember?"

"No, I don't remember that. Is this an emergency?"

"Sort of. It's time for the roller coaster snowball."

"The what?"

"The roller coaster snowball."

"What is the roller coaster snowball?"

"It's the snowball that hits you when you're on the roller coaster."

"Oh, that makes sense. Where are you going today, all dressed up like that?"

"Nowhere. I thought I'd pretend to go to work like everyone else and see how it feels. See people's reactions, how they react to me if they think I'm one of them. See if it's different from how they normally react."

"How do they normally react?" I asked, getting a little flustered.

"They don't react. That's just it, V, they don't react to me."

"Well, you're lucky," I said, trying to make light of the conversation. "It's better than if they react badly. Believe me, it's better."

"I don't know about that. I think a bad reaction is better than none at all. It's terrible not to be noticed. Shall I make dinner while you're at work?"

"Micky, I told you, I'm not going to work. I don't have my job anymore. I'm going to a few art stores to get some paints and canvases. I'm an artist now, remember?" There was something clearly wrong with my brother that morning.

"Oh, yeah, but when you get back, let's do something special, just the two of us. OK?"

"Sure. What do you have in mind?"

"I don't know. Let's see when the time comes. It'll be time and we'll know what to do. I can't wait, V. Thanks for breakfast. I've got to get to work."

He got up from the table, kissed me on the cheek, and headed out the front door in his suit and tie, joining the others who were on their way to their jobs. Something was seriously wrong and I wasn't sure I knew how to handle it.

I hoped that when I saw my brother later he would be back to normal. But we can hope for a lot of things. It was the beginning of a major turning point in our lives. A turning point that was inevitable, that would take us to where we are today.

CHAPTER FORTY-THREE: MICKY

I was having a great insight into my life. I was dressed like everyone else—men, that is. I wanted to see what it was like to wear the male costume of our time, these cravat things we wear around our necks, these respectable phallic protrusions: symbols of power, virility, and conformity.

I felt like I was choking on the absurdity of it all. I could hardly breathe. My throat chakra, if you will—my voice, my expression, my individuality—was choking. But it was an interesting experiment to be like everyone else. I assumed that most of them were stifled in their freedom of expression. I assumed that was why they went to work.

So I tried walking down the street with the rest of them, walking to the train. I felt very out of place: I forgot to bring an attaché case! Oh well, I thought, I still had the uniform.

It was quite an experience on the day I was ready to become myself. I walked down to the train station and waited for the train. The train to the big city. Everyone was reading their morning paper. They all wanted to keep abreast of the times. To know what was happening in the world. To feel important, to feel grown up.

The train arrived. I almost got on, but decided my little game had gone far enough. When the train was out of sight and no one was around, I tore off my tie and threw it on the train tracks. It felt so good, so releasing—so symbolic!

I had thrown off my tie of imprisonment and was starting to feel like a free man. There was just one more thing I had to do. It was very important and I had to go home and tell Viagra right away.

So I walked back to the house but her car wasn't there. I guessed she had gone to work like everyone else. Even my sister couldn't escape that necessity.

I felt Dave approaching and it would soon be time for us to meet him. I knew exactly where he would be. I felt it clearly.

As soon as Viagra came back from work I would tell her. I would make her take a walk with me. We would go out to meet our fate, to meet Dave, and all would be perfect in the world. I couldn't wait for her to get home. I couldn't wait for us to meet our fate.

I couldn't wait because I knew it was time.

It was time and it was good to know it.

CHAPTER FORTY-FOUR: VIOLET

When I returned from my art shopping, much later than I expected, Micky was lying on the living room floor. He seemed like he was in a trance. There was a smile on his face, reminiscent of those enlightened masters you see in newspaper ads, promising the secret wisdom of the ages.

I didn't want to disturb him because he looked so peaceful. He lay there with his suit still on, no tie, and his arms stretched out, as if he were high from contemplating the universe, which perhaps he was after all. His smile seemed all-knowing, like he'd finally found the answer, as if something had come to him that he'd been seeking for a long time. If this were true, who was I to interfere with it?

"Viagra...." he said quietly, sensing my presence in the room.

"Hi honey, are you OK?"

"More than OK, and you?" he asked, his eyes still closed.

"I'm good; I didn't want to disturb you."

"You could never disturb me, sweetheart. You are the opposite of a disturbance."

I didn't know what to say so I just gazed at my brother, in awe of who he was, fearful of what he might become. I wished I hadn't left him alone for so long. Immersed in my art shopping, the day had gone by without my realizing it.

We spent a long time in silence. I sat down on the couch and watched him. His eyes twitched like he was in the REM state of sleep, his long lashes fluttering like moths across a lamp; and he seemed to be in a deep reverie of some sort, something that was promising him a sense of revelation, a new kind of existence.

Suddenly he opened his eyes and looked right at me. He knew that

I was sitting on the couch. He beamed up at me with one of the most beautiful smiles I had ever seen on him, a sweet, deep smile; a smile from deep inside his consciousness.

I smiled back, happy that he seemed OK; and he said, "Let's go for a walk."

I paused for a second and asked, "Why?"

He paused himself and answered, "It's time."

And I felt no need to say, "Time for what?" Instead I trusted him and said, "All right. Let's go."

I walked over and gave him my hand to help him up. He leapt to his feet, as if I'd given him a lifeline; and he embraced me like a long lost lover from the past.

"Follow me," he said, taking my hand again and leading me out of the house.

We turned right and walked up the hill—and then down the hill by the train station. The passengers were coming back from work. We passed the houses of my neighborhood, then Main Street, the library, and the old school, being torn down that summer to make way for the new school around the corner, ready for the fall.

We walked farther and farther without saying a word to each other. Finally, my curiosity got the better of me and I asked, "Where are we going?"

"Do you really want to know? Or do you want to be surprised?"

"I think I'd like to know."

"Are you sure?"

"I think so."

"OK, V. We're going to Paris, to the *Champs Elysées*. There's a big surprise awaiting us there. I'm sure of it. And the timing's just about right. I can feel it. Can you feel it, V? Can you feel that certainty of fate all around us? Like something is about to happen? I can feel this feeling, honey. I know it's true. I don't want to tell you everything because I don't want to spoil the surprise, but we're going to see someone, someone special, someone we both know—and this will change everything, I'm sure. I don't know why, but I'm sure. And it will take us where we need

172

to go. So that everything becomes perfect for us."

His eyes had tears in them as he smiled at me, still holding my hand, pulling me in the direction of the boulevard. Something felt very right about this; it's hard to explain, like I knew we were doing the right thing somehow, as strange as it seemed.

We arrived at Elysian Boulevard as the sun began its decent over the western mountains. The clouds covering the sun formed a reddish-orange picture, like a volcano; and the rays shone out in all directions, as if the angels were about to appear and offer their gifts to us.

We stood there at the edge of the boulevard, looking at each other, watching the setting sun, and feeling the wind starting to blow.

Micky looked at his watch. "We may have to wait a little while," he said.

"I'm in no hurry," I said, not realizing how long we would have to wait. We were waiting for something...I didn't know what yet... something that promised to be...the answer for both of us? We waited and waited, we watched it getting darker, we saw the street lights going on one by one, and then the car lights going on. It looked like a postcard, with the cars approaching us shining white light and the cars driving away shining red. I felt like I was in love with my brother. He hadn't let go of my hand all that time.

Suddenly he pointed to the western mountains, now lit up with a golden haze.

"Look, V. Can you see it? Can you see it over there?"

"What am I looking for?" I asked.

"Can you see it? It's Dave—it's his truck—he's coming! He's coming!"

"Oh, yes, Micky. I can see a red truck up there. How do you know it's Dave's truck? How do you know he's coming?"

"I just know it, honey, I can feel it. I know it's him. I know it."

He was radiant. I had never seen my brother that way. His curly hair blew in the breeze and the glow around his head suspended him in time. It's an image I'll never forget; in fact, I'm planning to paint this portrait of him, this portrait of my brother: Micky in his final moments before the turning point.

"You're such a special brother, Micky."

"And you're my beautiful sister, V. Trust me."

And he led me by the hand. He led me across the boulevard, where the red light turned into pure white light...and he touched my face and said, "Viagra, if there's anything or anyone I love in this world, it's you, my darling."

And we stood in the white light and awaited our oncoming big red truck....

CHAPTER FORTY-FIVE: DAVE

Where the hell am I? I'm lost, I think. I never get lost. My boss is going to kill me. I'm very late. I'm somewhere in the mountains and I'm going around in circles. I can't seem to get out of here. Let me pull over and look at a map. I must've made a wrong turn somewhere.

OK—I'm retracing my steps. I turned off 99—I can see it here on the map—oh, I must've made this wrong turn onto Hedge Way. I was supposed to continue straight on till Elysian. Fuck. So what do I do now?

Well, it looks like if I follow this winding road here, I just might get out of this maze. OK, I'll try that.

It's starting to get dark. I can't believe it. I don't even know if I can do my delivery now. I'll probably lose my job over this. Well, maybe Shel will understand. Anyone can make a wrong turn. Maybe I've had enough of this job anyway. Things happen for a reason. Everything happens for a reason, you know?

Maybe Micky will let me spend the night at his place. I'm starved. I haven't had anything to eat. What a life this is. What the hell am I doing, anyway? Everything seems to be going wrong.

OK—enough complaining. Let's get going. I think if I follow this road around, it'll lead out of here to the boulevard. That's where I want to be. Hell, I don't even know how late this place is open. They've probably given up on me and gone home. And I wouldn't blame 'em. Who would wait around for me this long? Micky would, I bet. He's a good buddy. How many good buddies have I had in my life? Not that many.

Maybe I should call my office. Oh, there it is—finally—Elysian Boulevard. It's practically nighttime. What a fine mess I've made of everything. Well, everything happens for a reason, so maybe something else will happen, something unexpected. Yeah, right? Like what? I'm not in the greatest mood, in case you can't tell.

Lately I've been having the strangest sensation. Like my truck is driving itself, like it goes where it wants to go. Like it drives all by itself—and I'm just in here for decoration, you know? So people won't get weirded out, seeing a truck driving down the road with no driver in it. I know this is crazy, but it's almost what it feels like.

Like I know I wanted to go one way—to the boulevard, but the truck seemed to want to go up this winding road. Weird. I don't know how to explain it. I've been feeling pretty weird anyway, so what else is new? I'd like to finish this drive and settle in for a couple of brews, you know? That'd be nice. That's what I'd like to do. I'm exhausted.

All right. I'm on Elysian. Golly gee. I'm here and it only took me seven hours. I'm just a real pro. Oh yeah. OK, let's see the numbers. Nowhere near 123 yet, but it looks like it'll be on the right-hand side.

Look at that—I went to scratch my neck—and the truck is driving all by itself. I took my hands off the wheel, just for a second. Let me try it a little longer. Whoa. It seems to know where to go. It seems to know when to start and when to stop. Look at that! It stopped at a light. No it didn't—I put my foot on the brakes.

I think I'm just a little tired, a little weirded out. But sometimes I get the feeling like I'm not in control, you know? Like I'm an instrument of some higher force. Did you ever feel that way? Like you're a puppet, sort of, and someone else is pulling the strings? Sometimes I feel like it doesn't matter what I do, whatever I do, I'm going to end up in such and such a place, whether I turn left or whether I turn right. Like it doesn't matter. Like it's all planned out and I have no say about it.

There it goes again. Did I turn the wheel or did the truck change lanes all by itself? What the hell is happening with this truck anyway? I'm going to have to get the steering alignment checked out.

I still don't see 123. I'm a long way off. I've definitely missed this delivery. Let me turn on the radio. See what I get. Oh, there's a children's chorus singing:

Good men, let us pass

Conquer we shall Jerusalem
Guided by Gabriel's flaming flight
For we are God's own infantry
Give us your ships, give us the sea

Nice music. Seems like I've heard it somewhere before. Real nice, like the Middle Ages or something.

Music hypnotizes you, you know? Puts you in a kind of trance. Makes you drive on automatic pilot—like you don't have to do anything, like the truck does all the work. Now it sounds like the grown-ups are singing:

Behold the singing children
God's own little knights
Barefoot and ragged
And consumed with loneliness
They come toward us

Everything seems to be about God these days. Like there's this higher power that pulls our strings, our puppet strings. But I don't believe in that. I like to think I'm pulling my own strings.

What burning vision in their sunken eyes
Gave them such lasting strength?

Wow. This music is intense. I like that. I'm probably the only D.A. who likes classical music, but that's OK with me. It puts me under a spell, a driving spell.

Everything feels like it's happening in slow motion. Must be the music. Feels like a movie, a slow motion movie. All the headlights on my left are shining white light at me—all the taillights in front of me are beaming red. This is a dream, a magic spell. Hey, I see a number all lit up: there it is! 123! It's flashing up ahead! I'm reaching my destination!

It must be my imagination, part of the movie, but I think I see Micky and Viagra in the street up ahead, holding hands. Gotta be my imagination. Micky's waving at me—and Viagra's hair is changing colors. I'm getting closer to them. It's great to see them! I'll be able to give them a lift!

Wait a second...I'm getting closer to them. The music is taking me, the movie is taking me...all in slow motion...I'm trying to steer away from them...but my truck wants to go straight at them...NO...I'm steering away from them...*I'm* in charge here—*I'm* the driver! What a dream, what a vision! There's Micky, like he's really there...there's Viagra, as pretty as I remember her...I'm driving their way...I'm getting closer...they're not moving...they're waiting for me...they're waiting for me to...what? Hit them? Run them over? Like I did—

What was I thinking? I'm having flashes of something.

Like I did—

Their parents?

Doesn't make sense. How could I run over their parents? I must be losing my mind.

I'm getting flashbacks —

I feel like I remember—I feel like I can see it—I *did* run over their parents...I ran over a lot of people...I killed a little kid...I killed a lot of children. How can this be true? I just want to make people happy. I'm a good guy. I don't want to hurt anybody.

I'm getting closer to them. I'm getting very close. I'm going to hit them if I don't do something. If I don't do something right away. Hell, I'm stronger than this truck. I'm stronger than any strings that are trying to pull me. I'm not going to hit Micky and Viagra. I'm not. I'm not.

I'm turning my wheel to the right. I'm heading toward number 123. I know what I'm doing. I'm stronger than this truck. I'm stronger than any force of life—or death. *I'm* the strong one! *I'm* in charge!

With all my might and all my will power, I'm steering the truck to the right—I won't hit them, I won't—I don't want to kill anyone—

The truck is listening to me! It knows that I'm stronger! I'm winning! I'm not going to hurt Micky and Viagra! I'm making a sharp turn—I'm swerving—I'm going to crash into the building!—I'm CRASHING INTO IT!—the truck's EXPLODING!!!—I'm on fire! I'm on fire!

HELP ME! SOMEONE! I'M ON FIRE!

Let me get out of here. Fuck—the door won't open—I'm trapped— I'm locked in—I can't get out of here!

Jesus Christ. There's fire everywhere. I'm trying the door again. Oh, come on! It won't move! I'm stuck in here! Ahhhh, it's so hot—the fire's so close to me! But I'm remembering...I think I understand. I have been an instrument of a higher force, a force of God, a force of death. I have come from somewhere else, to take people away—to send them to their souls. That was my job—to send them to their souls.

But it's over now. Look at my body—I'm burning up! Look at my life—what was it all about? Killing people? No more—I've killed too many people. And now I've killed myself...for the two people I love. Ahhhh, Micky...it really hurts. Violet...please...understand....

The flames are all around me now. I'm a part of them. I can't breathe. But I'm not afraid. My name is Dave and I'm not afraid.

I leave this earth knowing that I did something right. I finally did something right. I disobeyed God to do what I knew was right.

CHAPTER FORTY-SIX: VIOLET

My name is Violet Shore and I am an artist. You may be familiar with my work, for it is shown all over the world. How did this happen? How did this evolve? You who have listened to my story know the answer; for it is in these pages that my talent was born: with Micky, Dave, and Max, the three men I have loved most in this world. If it weren't for them, I would never be the woman I am today.

I have other people to thank as well: my wonderful dealer Larry Kipper, who believed in me from the start; and Hans and Erda, with whom I finally made peace, having sent them a nice check after the sale of my first painting, *The Bath*. It has changed owners several times in the last few years and currently hangs in Stockholm at the *Moderna Museet*.

As I tour the world, attending my openings and lecturing to art students, I am often asked what it's like to be living the dream of a renowned artist. My answer is usually the same: you have to pay the price. Painting, or any art form, is not just a pleasant activity; it is a life choice, a choice that is willed with your blood.

In his *Gay Science*, Nietzsche says that the sensitive nature of animals, including their psychic ability, comes from their pain—and that people would like to have this power, not realizing the depth of suffering implicit in such a gift. It is the same with the artist. We are like sensitive animals: we pay the price for the art we create. I certainly did, as you who have followed my story know.

It all goes back to that deep place inside us, when we were little girls and little boys, needing to be accepted, needing to be loved. If a child yearns for these qualities, there are many possibilities for good or ill, the artist being one of them; but most great artists, it seems to me, have a leftover pain from childhood that needs to be healed through their art.

I am lucky to have had the satisfaction of painting all my ideas, including the ones I have mentioned to you; and the response from the public has been more than kind. People seem to understand what I am trying to say through my work. I am fortunate indeed and consider myself blessed.

Some of us have been less fortunate, though, my brother being one of them. I visit him whenever I can, whenever I am in the States; and we still share that special bond we always had. Yet a certain light seems to have faded from his eyes, ever since that fateful night on the boulevard, when Dave sacrificed his life for us.

I have painted the fire, the explosion, the truck going up in flames— you see, the blazing that night had the fascination it always had for me: whenever I witnessed a fiery disaster, I was always overwhelmed by the sheer beauty of it. So I decided to paint the fire.

It is one of my largest canvases, entitled simply, *Burning Truck*. And what's unusual about the painting is that you cannot see any truck at all, just the flames—and contained within, a very faint outline of a man, a heroic man, being burned to death.

What I find most intriguing about the painting, though, and perhaps you will agree if you ever see it, is what I chose to include in the bottom right-hand corner. This was, of course, what actually flew out of the truck at the time of its explosion. It's as if the entire contents of the trailer were hurled back onto the boulevard, not far from where Micky and I were standing:

The mirrors. Many large mirrors. I will never forget them, for they seem to solve a certain mystery about Dave and who he really was.

These were no ordinary mirrors that landed on the boulevard that night, safe from the fire and miraculously unbroken. I believe they are called "true mirrors," or "true reflection mirrors." Either way, they show your true reflection, as other people see you; not as you usually perceive yourself in an ordinary mirror. This is what Dave carried in his truck: mirrors that reveal your true self.

I first realized this as I walked toward the mirrors with Micky. I immediately noticed that my right hand, the hand that held Micky's, showed up on the left side of the mirror. The image was reversed; and yet it was the true image.

I looked at myself and had a very moving experience: amidst the flames and the sirens and the turmoil about us on the boulevard, for the first time in my life, I saw myself as beautiful. I don't mean in a vain way; I mean I saw an inner beauty that I had never seen before. And contrasted with the drama around me, it gave me a great sense of peace. I was overcome with emotion.

My brother, however, seemed to have the opposite reaction. He looked at himself in the true mirror—and I believe this was the real turning point for him—for his hair became completely white. Right before my eyes! I thought it was something to do with the fire at first; but his hair has stayed that way ever since. There was a terror in his eyes from the moment he saw himself; and I have never known him to be the same.

It's not anything he said; it's what he didn't say. He opened his mouth wide, wider—and screamed without sound. The anguish of his soul was released at that moment; and I don't remember ever seeing a more terrifying sight, even more terrifying than the flames, the police cars, the fire trucks, and the knowledge of what happened to Dave.

It was during these moments that I knew my brother had left the world—the world that you and I know, anyway—and went to live somewhere else. It's the saddest thing I have ever known—and I have known my share of sad things.

He was silent for a long time after seeing the mirrors, but then he ran toward the fire and started yelling, "Dave! Dave! Come back! Dave!"

He was quite hysterical and I tried to calm him down, but to no avail. I had to take him away after that and bring him to the place where he lives now. He seems somewhat content there; he assures me he is very happy; but he does so without speaking verbally. He writes down his thoughts on paper or types them on the computer they have there. He has not uttered one audible word since his last "Dave! Dave! Come back! Dave!" It breaks my heart to think of it; and I try to visit him as often as I can.

For when you see your true reflection, your true image, without artifice, without deception, you will either be at peace or at war with yourself. Yet who am I to assume that Micky is at war with himself? Perhaps he has found his own peace after all; perhaps he has found God. This is what he claims—and who am I to question it?

The true reflection—that is what Dave delivered all along. Some of us can deal with it, some of us can't. But once you see your true reflection, I don't think life is ever the same.

Max was glad that I made peace with Hans and Erda; he still lives there and refuses to leave, the stubborn man! And who am I to convince him otherwise? He's happy there, he says, and that's his choice, his home. Although my relations with the Colony are much improved, I don't feel comfortable going back, especially with the fame I now know.

So Max and I write long letters and emails and talk on the phone occasionally. It's a life-long friendship and we will always stay in touch. But it's important that you don't wish us a Hollywood happy ending. Please don't wish us that. That's not what life is really about—and you know it. Life is about struggle; it's about learning who you are.

In any case, as I've intimated before, it's Dave whom I consider to be my greatest love, as different as we were. If it weren't for his not contacting me, I would never have gone to the Colony; and if it weren't for his sacrifice, I would never be alive today. At least that's how I see it: for it looked like he was about to hit us that night, as we stood on the island in the center of the boulevard—but at the last second he swerved away, creating the colorful scene that is now my painting. Perhaps he knew after all, although he never admitted it to us, what he carried in his truck. Perhaps the self-knowledge that he carried made him a deeper person than he appeared to be.

None of us will ever know for sure. All I know is that Dave was the kind of man I will never meet again. Late at night before falling asleep, I often wish that I could meet him in my dreams, that I could see the red truck again; but in all these years, I don't remember having this experience. Those dreams are now a thing of the past; and perhaps it's best to be rid of them.

They say that we are condemned to repeat our past until we understand it. And I don't claim to have full knowledge of everything, but there is something eerie about Dave's truck being so similar to the one that killed my parents; and something surely seems to be released now that Dave and his truck are gone. There are many symbols of life and death that are beyond our comprehension; all we can do is realize that they exist—and not be overly pat or certain in our interpretation of them.

For it just may turn out that a truck driver has more understanding than an educated man; or that an educated man has less integrity than his own words written on a rock somewhere high in the hills.

I have seen much of life and I paint what I see. I try not to judge it; I try to paint it as it is. I try to get to the truth, like a mirror that shows us the true reflection of ourselves.

As I said when I was a little girl, "If I can paint a beautiful painting, that's all that matters to me."

Anything else is superfluous; yet I'll take happiness when it comes.

CHAPTER FORTY-SEVEN: MICKY

They have a beautiful garden here where I'm staying. It's very large—more like a giant backyard. There's a huge maple tree in the center of it—and in the fall its leaves turn bright red, my favorite color.

But now it's summer again; I've spent several summers here, I think. And don't tell anyone, because they probably wouldn't believe you, but I am very happy here. I actually love it here except for a few minor points, like the television-watching slobs who monopolize the activity room in the evening, when I need to concentrate on typing my latest chapter for you.

I've got a nice room which I've decorated with my collection of rocket ships and toy trucks; and over my bed is the portrait Viagra painted of me, all aglow on the boulevard. I don't remember it happening exactly, but Viagra assures me that it did; and I'm lucky to have such a good-looking picture of myself, before my hair changed colors.

Viagra's a famous artist, you know. She has shown me pictures of all her paintings—and I am just amazed. I'm in awe of my beautiful, talented sister. She's a genius, you know. A real genius. I love her more than anyone in this world, but I can tell she doesn't believe me when I say how happy I am here. Nobody believes us really, but what do we care? Some of us are happier than we've ever been in our lives. And why shouldn't we be? We live in this gorgeous hotel, have pretty good meals, and share a wonderful life together. I could do without the television noise; and I wish they played more classical music; but other than that, there's not much to complain about. It's a good life.

But don't let me deceive you. I know what most people think. I even know what *you're* thinking. You see, I haven't lost my ability to read your mind. I know what you're thinking right now! That I'm crazy, right?

Hah! I guessed it! No, I *knew* it!

Well, you can call me what you like—it's only a word. A word, perhaps, that you feel comfortable using. A word to classify my state of mind so that you can feel comfortable with yours—and comfortable with your notion of who I am. But I don't care what words you use; I've already told you that I don't like to be sane because I am *in*sane—and I enjoy it!

Seriously, though, because I'm a serious guy, I am aware of the general consensus, the general opinion on the folks who live here. But did you ever stop to wonder what we might think about you? You over there in the normal world? Bet you didn't think of that, did you? That's OK, don't worry about it. I'm just playing around with you. I'm in a good mood today, like most days, and I'm just playing around.

But now I want to get serious and tell you some serious stuff, OK? But please don't tell anyone. This is just between us, OK?

We have a secret society here: those of us who have found the answer, those of us who have found our form of God. We meet once a week in the garden and compare our experiences. Most of us have given up talking in everyday life, but we save our verbal communication for these meetings. Why waste words unless there's something important to say?

And we do feel our meetings are important. Sometimes we don't talk, though; sometimes we have rituals and sacrifice wine to the gods. We're allowed to have wine here. We're allowed to do practically whatever we want. And our weekly get-togethers are some of the best times I've known. But they're top secret—the authorities know nothing about our meetings—so please don't tell them; they think we're reading poetry or something like that. Well, we do read Yeats from time to time; but not for the reasons you think.

How did we find each other, you may ask. Good question. We found each other by that special look in our eyes. That look of the Great Beyond. You can just tell if someone is a brother or sister. You can tell if someone is one of us.

I enjoy our weekly meetings and I enjoy most of the people who attend them. We have men and women, young and old. It's quite satisfying, I assure you. But the major joy I have is alone in my room, listening to music, and experiencing contact with a higher world, which is very difficult to put into words.

It's moments like these that are sacred to me; and I want to tell you more about them. But first, there is something very special in my room that I found one day; and I'd like to tell you the story of how I found it.

One sunny day about a year ago, I jumped over the hedges surrounding the garden and decided to go for a walk. We're allowed to leave from time to time, as long as we don't get into any serious trouble; and something seemed to be calling me in an eastward direction; so I "jumped the hedges," as we say here, and started walking east.

As I said, it was a beautiful sunny day; I think it was in June—and the May blossoms had given way to more elegant greenery as the first day of summer drew near. I started walking eastward, not knowing where I was going or what to expect; but I had learned to trust my hunches, and knew that there must have been a good reason for my walk.

I passed a plain, white church, its steeple rising up to an empty sky; I passed a supermarket with a parking lot full of housewives' cars; I passed a post office, a bank, a video store—and I kept walking as the sun shone directly over my head and said to me out loud: "Micky, it is time to turn right."

So I listened to the sun's voice, turned right, and where should I find myself but the local junkyard. I had never been to a junkyard before, and at first I found it to be quite a mundane type of place to visit. But I trusted the voice of the sun and decided to peruse the junkyard and see what I could find there.

I felt pulled in a particular direction; I could feel this force pulling me. And suddenly I realized why I was called to the junkyard. On top of a heap of rusted metal was something I recognized. My right arm rose up by itself and slowly reached out to grab it, as if it were a vision I had to grasp before it disappeared. It was Raven's rear-view mirror. I swear it was. I recognized it right away, not only because it was black and looked exactly like Raven's mirror; but after all these years, it still had two rocket ships dangling from it. The red color had faded a bit from the rockets, but it was definitely Raven's rear-view mirror; so I reached out to grasp it, as I said, like grasping a memory. And instead of disappearing, it was very real in my hand.

Knowing this was the reason for my journey that day, I took the mirror with me and headed back home. It was a very fine day indeed; and I was happy to have Raven's mirror with me. I jumped back over the hedges and went straight to my room. I fastened the mirror to my wall underneath the portrait of myself and started gazing into it.

And it was astounding what I could see in this mirror. I could see anything I wanted to see from my past. It was truly a rear-view mirror! I saw Viagra, and Dave, and my parents, and my old girlfriend; I even saw Raven and the time the two of us drove to the desert! I saw the cactuses and could hear the country and western music. I watched many things with delight that first day I looked into the mirror. I even saw myself looking into some other mirror on some other day long before that—I couldn't remember when. There was fire behind me. It was like Moses and the Burning Bush, except there was no bush. It was a very profound experience, that much I realized.

I looked into the rear-view mirror and saw myself looking into this other mirror; and in that mirror, the whole world was a mirror: my mind was a mirror and my eyes were mirrors. And I heard a voice—I could hear it again inside my room—and the voice said, "Micky, look within your soul and know that you are God, just as everyone is God, and know that you have the power to see everything, to see all, to see the Great Beyond."

The voice was terrifying but it also was wonderful and I opened my mouth wide, wider—and screamed without sound; but I wasn't really screaming; I was really laughing—I was really singing—with great joy, with great exuberance, because I had finally found myself and had found God and realized we were the same.

And that was when I started to hear the voices coming out of the mirror, out of the fire, and out of the heaven above me. The voices of my past, the voices of the little boys and girls at school who sang with me, who laughed with me, who teased me for being different, who praised me, who cajoled me, who cried with me and played with me. I could hear them all, these voices from my past. I still hear them now, whenever I want to hear them. But they no longer scare me; they are soothing to me now. Because I know that all these voices are really the voices of God; and they are all a part of me; and I feel one with them, one with myself, and happy. I have never been happier.

And that is really all I have to tell you. It's nearly ten o'clock according to the cardinal, and that's when they kick us out and send us back to our rooms. There aren't any television watchers here tonight. I'm alone actually. They must have known; they must have intuited that it was a special night for me, finishing my story on the computer here.

I hope you have enjoyed listening to it. I've enjoyed telling it to you, but it's no big deal. And anyway, you've probably guessed that I made up the whole thing, that all the characters are really me...or are they?

It's just that I had nothing better to do today—that's really the truth. And if truth be told, as it so rarely is, I simply wanted to amuse myself—and you—with the true story of how I escaped from this world. This world of metaphors, similes, boulevards and rocket ships. Tomatoes and women with many different shades of hair.

And red toy trucks, big and powerful—as powerful as the imagination!—that lead us into a world where we can be free.

ACKNOWLEDGEMENTS

The night I saw the words "Sven Davisson" in my Gmailbox, I knew my life had changed. Sven took on the manuscript when no one else dared and published my short story too. Thanks Sven, it means a lot.

Also in the literary world, Janet Reid set me on the right track, James Fitzgerald offered excellent suggestions, Jennifer Lyons gave me a good deal of encouragement, and Christopher Schelling helped to get the ball rolling.

My buddies at Tahuti Lodge always, always encouraged me to do my will. 93, you guys. Andrea Lowencopf, I could never have done it without your early morning emails. Meri Axinn and Angel Millar gave me invaluable ideas in the first draft days. Rob Osonitsch gave me sanity in an insane world. Judy Kaufman, my toughest critic (and mother) forced me to get the dialogue right. Dan Maksimik and his not-so-big red truck gave me the friendship I needed during my loneliest times. And finally, my nephew who years ago, when asked who should tell the bedtime story, said: "Let Uncle Kyler do it—he's good at that." Thanks Jake, it helped me to go on.

www.ingramcontent.com/pod-product-compliance
Lightning Source LLC
Chambersburg PA
CBHW020647260626
47157CB00008B/2935